"I never gave a minute's thought to marrying you. How could I possibly?" Pamela's voice was breathless and uncertain.

His head inclined toward hers, and his voice lowered to a whisper. "If it is your indeterminate sort of half engagement to Nigel . . ."

"I wouldn't "

He silence n as a tentativ ssion as his ar

His assault stirred visions of a delightfully disreputable future. It was obvious a man who kissed like Lord Breslau had no notion of respectability. Pamela forgot all her mother's injunctions on the proper behavior of a young lady, as she returned every scandalous embrace.

Also by Joan Smith
*Published by Fawcett Books:*

# DRURY LANE DARLING

## Joan Smith

FAWCETT CREST • NEW YORK

A Fawcett Crest Book
Published by Ballantine Books
Copyright © 1988 by Joan Smith

Library of Congress Catalog Card Number: 88-91173

ISBN 0-449-21500-8

Manufactured in the United States of America

First Edition: November 1988

# DRURY LANE DARLING

# Chapter One

It was mid-January, and a raw wind nipped at Pamela Comstock's nose as she strode through the park toward Belmont. The scene before her was composed in shades of gray: gray stone house with windows rising up the front like great ladders, while a series of dormers and gables enlivened the roofline. Darker gray skeletons of trees clawed the silver sky. It looked like an etching in a gothic novel. Why the Raleigh's house should be called Belmont was one of life's less interesting mysteries. It was not particularly handsome, nor was it situated on any elevation that could conceivably be called a mount. The icy water squelching underfoot suggested Belmarsh might be a more appropriate name.

Miss Comstock was only a visitor at this Elizabethan heap, but if certain parents had their way she would become a tenant for life. The scion of the family, Nigel Raleigh was probably as tired of hearing hints dropped as she was herself, and as disinterested in the scheme. That was all that made these visits bearable; Nigel wasn't the slightest bit interested in her.

1

It added a certain cachet to her reputation at home in Kent to have a suitor lurking in the background. Her papa often pointed out that a lady of plain appearance and moderate fortune, fast advancing into her twenties, could not be too choosy. She did not intend to marry Nigel Raleigh, but that was her own affair.

A particularly persistent breeze found its way under her pelisse, and Pamela ran the last few yards to the safety of the front door. Lady Raleigh had told her, with that hopeful, maternal, coy look she knew and loathed, that Nigel should be arriving around three. It was now three-thirty. Pamela didn't think he had arrived yet, or she would have seen his carriage in the park. Nigel's arrival was of only marginal interest to her. It was his guest that had Pamela and the rest of the house in a flutter.

"Is she here yet?" she asked the butler when he opened the door to admit her.

"Not yet, Miss Comstock. Sir Aubrey and Lady Raleigh are in the saloon awaiting the marquise's arrival."

Pamela shivered out of her pelisse and round bonnet and handed them to Wetmore. A glance in the mirror showed her she looked a perfect fright, and she tidied her hair before entering the saloon.

"No sign of them yet," Lady Raleigh announced, and drew an impatient sigh. Lady Raleigh was a great one for sighs. She wore an habitual expression of being hard done by. Her favorite color was gray, to match her surroundings. Her brown hair had obligingly taken on the same hue as her dove-colored gown.

One could hardly blame Sir Aubrey for his occasional flings with a livelier female companion. There was nothing gray about him. His hair was still a rich brown, just turning to silver around the temples. No doubt the extremely dashing jacket of blue Bath cloth and the striped waistcoat he wore had been donned to honor the expected guest.

His blue eyes twinkled when he said, "The Marquise de Chamaude, eh? Nigel is up to all the rigs."

His lady gave him a jaundiced stare. "You don't want to encourage him in this freakish sort of behavior, Aubrey. Bringing an actress—and a French actress at that—to Belmont."

"Why, actresses are considered unexceptionable in France. The very fact that she married a marquis should tell you that, Dot."

"If she ever *did* marry one," his lady retorted sharply. "It seems odd to me that every Frenchie one runs across should be a member of the old aristocracy. It is pretty easy to claim a title in a foreign country."

Pamela listened, and in an effort to change the subject said, "The Flawless Fleur, they call her in London. Her Christian name is Fleur, I believe."

"Whoever heard of calling a child *Flower*," Lady Raleigh demanded in a purely rhetorical spirit. "And while it may be permissible for a lady to trot the boards in Paris, Aubrey, that does *not* make it appropriate in England. You should have written to Nigel forbidding the visit."

"The marquise is an eminent actress."

"An eminent nobody."

"We can put up with her for two days for the sake of Nigel's future," Sir Aubrey said placatingly. "It was a great coup for him to get the job of editing her

3

memoirs. The lad wants a literary career. This book may be the making of him."

"More likely the unmaking. If Colchester wanted to do the life of an actress, why did he not choose our own Tragic Muse, Mrs. Siddons?"

"She is old hat," Sir Aubrey said dismissingly. "Retired now. It is time London claim the marquise as the new star."

"A comedienne," his wife scoffed. Her glare told the room her opinion of comedy. "Your ancestors would roll over in their graves if they knew what sort of creature we were entertaining." She turned her darkling gaze to Pamela. "I shall write an apology to your mama for having you here at this time, my dear. If I had had the least notion . . ."

"I'm sure that's not necessary," Pamela said.

"Why, everybody and his dog was vying to entertain Mrs. Siddons when her husband died," Sir Aubrey pointed out. "There was even a rumor afoot she was engaged to Lord Erskine."

"No one ever heard the rumor he married her," his wife riposted.

"You'll hear no rumor of Nigel offering for the marquise, either, Dot, if that is what has your hackles up."

Lady Raleigh's eyes snapped and a spot of color invaded her sallow cheeks. "Marry her! I should hope not indeed. Nigel is engaged to Pamela. Furthermore, the hussy is ancient. She's been in England since the French Revolution, if rumor is to be believed."

"She still plays the ingenue exceedingly well," Sir Aubrey said. "I saw her in a revival of *The Provok'd Husband.*"

4

"I don't wonder he was provoked, if she played the wife," his wife snipped, and rearranged her shawls against the draft.

Belmont had all the amenities of a roundhouse. Smoking grates, drafty doors and windows, inedible food, and poor company.

Pamela went to the fire, ostensibly to warm her toes and fingers, but in truth she just wanted to escape the bickering of this tiresome couple. There was nothing as wearisome as a loveless match. Why had these two agreed to marry each other? It must have been an arranged marriage—of the sort her parents and Nigel's wished to force on them. Her determination not to have Nigel didn't require strengthening, but if it had, this would do it.

Twice a year her parents sent her on the fifty-mile jaunt from Chatham in Kent to Hertfordshire to visit her godmother, with a stopover to visit her Aunt Foster in London. She'd been coming for four years, and twice a year Nigel repaid the visit. Four years, sixteen visits. She had watched Nigel grow from an obstreperous university student to a foppish man-about-town. Now she would see him as a working gentleman. She knew in her heart she would still find him a fool, and he would find her a bore. Recognizing Nigel for a fool required no assistance, but she took some pains to ensure that he found her a bore.

It probably hadn't been necessary to wear her dullest gown and have her curly hair pulled back in a knot for this visit. Naturally Nigel would be infatuated with the infamous French actress. Although he favored his mother in appearance, his character had the unsteadiness of the Raleighs where petticoats were concerned. A smile curved Pamela's lips as she gazed into the leaping flames. Wouldn't it be exciting if Nigel actually offered for the Flawless Fleur! Lady Raleigh would have hysterics.

A second thought soon showed Pamela that the more likely gentleman to succumb to the marquise's mature charms was Sir Aubrey. He had already seen her perform. Did he, by any chance, know the lady personally? She wished to ascertain this without asking the question, and when Lady Raleigh went to speak to the servants, she returned to her chair.

"What does the marquise look like at close range, Sir Aubrey? she asked. "Is she terribly beautiful?"

"I've never seen her close up," he said sadly. "I went to the greenroom one night—no need to mention it to my lady—but the crowd around her was so tight I could hardly get a glimpse. She has hair the color of butter taffy. That's all I could see, for she's a statuesque lady. If I could convince Dot to live in London . . ."

The speech remained unfinished. Everyone who knew Lady Raleigh knew her aversion to living in the vice center of the universe. It was Sir Aubrey's one delight that when business took him thither, he went unaccompanied by Lady Raleigh. He found frequent excuses to see his man of business, but he had not found opportunity to be presented to the marquise. She was not interested in the acquaintance of a country squire bearing only the title of Sir Aubrey. Princes and dukes hung at her skirts.

The Flawless Fleur wore not only an aura of glamour, but one of vulnerability and fortitude as well. She had miraculously escaped Paris and the guillotine by hiding in a vegetable cart, like all the best heroines. A fishing vessel had carried her from France to dump her at the Prince Regent's doorstep at Brighton. Alone and destitute (her husband had been caught and executed in the Revolution, and the family fortune remained behind), she refused the formal protection of several married gentlemen and resumed her career as an actress instead.

The marquise was known to have had an occasional *affaire de coeur*—she was French after all—but she did not accept the formal protection of any of the illustrious aristocrats who were eager to bestow it. It took a few years before her heavily accented speech was comprehensible to dull English ears. She played the provinces first, but recently she had made it to Drury Lane, and her star was rising rapidly.

"You don't actually know Lady Chamaude then," Pamela said.

"Not yet," Sir Aubrey said impatiently, and drew out his turnip watch once more. "Did Dot tell you we are having another guest for the weekend?" he asked. He found Miss Comstock nearly as dull as his wife, but felt an obligation to entertain a guest.

"No," she said, and looked with curiosity to hear the name. Pamela guessed from the sulky set of his lips that the guest was some spinster aunt or cousin, of which Lady Raleigh was supplied with an infinite number.

"Breslau will be coming with them," he said curtly.

Pamela blinked in astonishment. Lord Breslau was a name often encountered in the journals. She had never met him personally, nor ever expected to. The Marquess of Breslau was a gentleman from the very tip of the *ton*. His most recent fame was connected

7

with Drury Lane, where he had been appointed a director of the committee after the fire of 1809, in hope that he might magically dissipate the enormous debt incurred by the rebuilding. And he was coming here, to Belmont.

"I expect he is a friend of the marquise's?" she asked.

"Bosoms bows. It was Breslau who discovered the marquise, when she was acting in the provinces. He takes an active interest in the theater, especially in Lady Chamaude's career. She is his protégée, you see. Breslau is some kin to my family. He's been keeping an eye on Nigel in London for us. He was instrumental in getting the lad assigned to writing the marquise's memoirs."

Sir Aubrey felt Nigel had asked Breslau along to dilute the sin of inviting the marquise. He was out in his reckoning. It hadn't softened the blow where Dot was concerned, and robbed half his own enjoyment of the visit. Obviously Breslau wouldn't have accepted an invitation to this rural backwater unless he was having an affair with the Flawless One. Sir Aubrey had no low opinion of his own charms, but he also knew hard competition when he met it.

"I see." Pamela nodded. This much-dreaded visit had taken on an air of wonderful excitement, and even intrigue. She read Sir Aubrey's thoughts quite easily. It soon occurred to her, however, that the marquise's affair with Breslau would leave Nigel completely free. She must look lively, or she'd have to spend time with him.

She was interrupted from her thoughts by the clatter of wheels approaching. Like Sir Aubrey, she darted to the window and saw a dashing black carriage with a lozenge on the door flying up the drive. Several cases were strapped to the top. The driver pulled four matched bays to a halt, and a liveried footman bounced down to open the door.

The first to exit was Nigel. A many-caped coat didn't fool Pamela regarding his figure. Hard to believe that under that yardwide of capes there sloped a pair of slender shoulders and a scrawny chest. The curled beaver hat would come off to reveal blond hair, nattily cut à la Brutus, but with the wispy, evanescent fineness of an infant's first hirsute growth.

Her attention quickened as Nigel handed down the marquise. Lady Raleigh chose that inconvenient moment to return.

"Ah, they are here!" she exclaimed, and Pamela had to turn from the window to reply, leaving the field to Sir Aubrey.

"Let us take a seat," her hostess suggested. "She'll see us gawking at the window. I wouldn't give the creature the notion we are the least bit curious. What was she wearing, Pamela?" she asked eagerly.

"A feathered bonnet and sables," Pamela replied, wiping all admiration from her voice.

Lady Raleigh gave a *tsk* of disgust at such ostentation. Before more could be said, they heard the butler opening the door, and Nigel's fluting voice sounded.

## Chapter Two

"The place don't look nearly so shabby in summer," Nigel was assuring the actress. "Every place looks dismal in winter, but in April it looks quite decent, don't it, Wes?"

A murmur of assent told them Lord Breslau was also in the door.

"It is charming," the actress assured him.

Lady Raleigh's features sharpened at the French accent. Sir Aubrey's face assumed the expression of a hungry dog at the smell of meat, and Pamela stared expectantly toward the doorway. There was a slight delay and a murmur of voices beyond the door while outer clothing was removed. The first to appear, and alone, was the marquise, who always liked to make a grand entrance. The occupants of the room stared as the apparition swept a graceful curtsy, smiled, and advanced with two white, jeweled hands outstretched.

Pamela stared with an open curiosity that soon turned to admiration. How could anyone possibly not love this wonderful person? She had never seen anyone so glamorous and charming. The marquise's bonnet had been removed to reveal the butter-taffy hair arranged in fashionable swirls and loops. Pamela's hand went automatically to her own outmoded do. She always wore it skimmed back when she visited Belmont, to quench Nigel's ardor. She thought of her new rose gown hanging in her closet in Kent. She should have been told the marquise was coming.

Pamela had thought the word *flawless* applied to the lady's acting, but she began to wonder if it wasn't a tribute to her beauty instead. Her complexion was pale and clear, her eyes large, dark, lustrous, and smiling. Her cheekbones were high and her chin was firm. Or so it looked at a glance across the room. Her full but lithe figure was encased in a traveling suit that not even Lady Raleigh could find a fault with, hard as she tried. It was dark green sarcenet, with a white fichu that added an air of innocence and a paisley shawl that added nothing, but would be welcome in the chilly saloon.

"Welcome to Belmont, madam," Sir Aubrey said, and bounced forward, eyes glazed with admiration, to seize her hand and pump it, while his wife's nostrils quivered in distaste.

While he told the marquise how much he had enjoyed her performance in *The Provok'd Husband,* Pamela took a quick glance at the others. Nigel looked even less appealing than usual. His nose was red at the end and his blue eyes were watering from the cold.

The famous Lord Breslau proved to be a tall, slender gentleman who needed no title to tell the world he was an aristocrat. He fairly reeked of it. Nothing but years of inbreeding could produce a nose so razor-thin, eyes so bored, a mouth so cynical, and an air of such perfect disinterest that it avoided arrogance by a hair. No one but Weston could have fashioned the superfine jacket that sat like a second skin on his shoulders. His dark brown hair was worn short, brushed back in protest against the popular Brutus do.

His manners, she allowed, were excellent. He proceeded straight to Lady Raleigh, bowed, and assured her her son was doing excellently in London. There was a general commotion of introducing everyone.

The marquise proclaimed herself *enchantée* to meet Mees Calmstock. Pamela smiled and returned the compliment. Her bright eyes did not fail to observe, however, that at this close range the crow's work was visible at the corners of the marquise's eyes. The neck, too, while firm, was beginning to assume the texture of crepe.

Lord Breslau was "charmed" to meet Miss Comstock, and said, "Nigel has told me so much about you." Nigel, he noticed, had not been quite accurate in his description. He said the girl was "a great dull lump of a country bumpkin Mama plans to foist on me." She was actually a rather small dull lump. When the introductions were over, there was a polite search for seats.

Lady Raleigh had no intention of sharing a sofa with an actress, and with a commanding beam from her eyes, she impelled Nigel and Pamela to the sofa, one on either side of her. This left the marquise abandoned to Sir Aubrey's eager company. Under Dot's steely gaze, he showed her to a chair and pulled his own chair as close as he dared. Lord Breslau took up a pose by the fireplace, with one booted foot on the grate and half of his back to the room.

In deference to the company, the talk turned to drama as soon as the trip had been covered and the observation made that they were lucky to have beat the rain.

"We are just paying you a dashing visit," the marquise said. "The tyrant"—she glanced playfully at Lord Breslau—"has given me two nights off. I must be back in London for Wednesday's performance."

"We have an unexceptionable replacement in Rose Flanders," Breslau said. This earned him an angry flash from the marquise.

"How are you making out with clearing the debt at Drury Lane?" Lady Raleigh enquired politely of Breslau. Thus far, she had nodded to the actress, but not actually spoken to her.

"Lady Chamaude's performances are always sold out," Breslau replied, with what the hostess considered a quite unnecessary acknowledging bow to the actress.

The marquise, who found Sir Aubrey every bit as dull as he feared, lent an ear to the other conversation. "Give me a real role and you will see a real performance," she snipped.

"By Jove, I saw a real performance when I went to watch you," Sir Aubrey assured her.

"The marquise is referring to tragedy," Breslau informed them. "It's a cliché in the theater that actors always want to perform the roles they're least qualified for."

Lady Raleigh stirred to life. "Lady Chamaude plays the ingenue, I believe?" she remarked, addressing her words to the grate.

There was a short, uncomfortable silence, finally broken by the marquise, who exercised her control not to hear that spiteful remark. "You think I couldn't play tragedy?" she challenged Breslau. Fire darted from her fine dark eyes. "How is the world to know I can act, if I am only allowed to laugh and flirt? I have known much tragedy in my life, as Sonny could tell you. It is all in my memoirs."

Lady Raleigh bridled up to hear Nigel being called a pet name by this creature.

"In the dull months, folks want comedy," Breslau insisted. "Our tragedies never fare half so well."

"They would if Fleur was playing the lead," Nigel said staunchly. Lady Raleigh's nostrils pinched in chagrin.

"Is *MacBeth* not a tragedy?" the actress asked. "It did very well at Covent Garden last season."

Pamela noticed that Breslau and his flirt were enjoying a lovers' spat, and conjured with how this might affect her visit vis-á-vis Nigel.

"None of the chairs left the hall," Breslau allowed with one of his bored looks, and turned his attention to the fire, to try to kick the embers to flame.

Pamela wished to store up some anecdotes to take home as trophies to Kent and said to the marquise, "I read that you escaped from the guillotine in a cabbage cart, Lady Chamaude. Is it true?"

"*Non*, it was a cart full of rutabagas," she replied, and told the oft-repeated story of this hair-raising experience, with a sword being plunged into the vegetables, missing her by inches. Her gown was slit from the blade, just the way Pamela had read.

"It's all in chapter two," Nigel said, for he had

14

heard the story several times and wanted to discuss his own editing of the memoirs instead.

"I look forward to reading it," Sir Aubrey said. "It should make a dandy tale."

Breslau looked over his shoulder. "You won't want to miss it, Aubrey. You were one of Prinney's set in those days, I think. Perhaps you remember the French refugees landing at Brighton?"

"I recall some talk of it."

"The Prince Regent himself pulled me from the lugger and placed his mantle over me," Lady Chamaude said, her eyes glowing. "He put some of us up at his Brighton pavilion. I fear he is a naughty man, but I shan't mention that in my memoirs. Noblesse oblige," she added.

"But that was years ago!" Pamela exclaimed. "You must have been a child, Lady Chamaude."

"Oh, a *veritable enfant*, though I was married. We marry very young in France." This was the trickiest portion of the memoirs, to account for having been married and on the stage while still more or less in pinafores. The landing at Brighton had occurred over two decades ago, and the Marquise disliked to admit to much more than thirty years. "Ladies marry much later in England, of course," she added with a meaningful glance at Miss Comstock, still single. That would teach the bright-eyed chit to do her arithmetic in public.

Help came from an unlikely quarter. "I wouldn't put much past some of Prinney's set," Lady Raleigh said grimly. She had managed to cut her husband off entirely from those rakehell friends. "I remember hearing some pretty scandalous stories about the

15

carrying on at Brighton." Aubrey was right in the thick of it, too, but she'd soon brought *that* to a halt.

"The dear prince is a changed man now," the marquise said. She enjoyed his favor, and had no intention of embarrassing him in her memoirs. "He was a very model of kindness to me in those days. He let me ride a pretty white pony. I called her Lady Blanche, and placed three white plumes under her crown piece—the Prince of Wales's feathers, you know."

No one noticed the sudden frown that assailed Sir Aubrey's features. The incident stirred dormant memories. There had been a French refugee taken under Prinney's wing in those days. Corinne was her name, like the heroine of Madame de Staël's novel. A pretty, brown-eyed, brown-haired little filly she was, full of pep and vinegar. The marquise, he assumed, had heard the story and used it. Corinne would be nudging forty by now. The marquise didn't look a day over thirty.

His eyes slid to her profile as she regaled the company with other Brighton tales. "Oh, they were all a naughty bunch of boys." She laughed gaily. "I remember one—I called him my groom, because he always accompanied me when I rode Lady Blanche in the Marine Parade." She turned and cast a sapient eye on Sir Aubrey. "Perhaps you remember him, Sir Aubrey?"

Sir Aubrey looked, and felt the hair on the back of his neck lift. How Corinne had changed! Her hair had magically turned to a soft blondish red. Her maidenly body had filled out majestically. Her voice, her manner—all were different, but the eyes were the same. She still had those sharp, knowing eyes.

"Can't say that I do," he said gruffly.

She smiled demurely. "Perhaps my visit will jog your memory. It is one of the reasons I'm here," she threatened sweetly. "Nigel told me you were in Brighton at that time. I'm eager to meet old friends and refresh my own memory. You'd be surprised what talking over the old days can bring up. Lord Alban, for instance, has been most helpful."

Alban! Yes, he'd been after Corinne as well! Ho, they were all after her. But she'd favored himself. Not as rich as the others, but more handsome. Dot had been home at Belmont that spring. Nigel was only a few months old. How it all came washing back. Corinne, the little cottage at Freshfield Place, near the park. Then the summons from Dot. "Come home at once if you ever want to see your son again." Who had told her? Alban's work, very likely.

Had Alban replaced him? He had recently been "most helpful." There was a very sly glint in Corinne's eye when she said that. Was it posssible she was here to hold him to ransom? Pay up, or I reveal you in my book for the scoundrel you are? "Alban, you say? I haven't seen him in an age."

"He is still very dashing—like you, Sir Aubrey. He comes to all my plays. We'll talk later, *non*? I'm sure you will remember some helpful details for my memoirs. All my old friends are very generous in assisting me."

The marquise smiled her charming, warm smile, and turned her attention to Lady Raleigh. No amount of praising the ugly old house turned the termagent up sweet. "I saw a lovely Palladian bridge over a stream as we drove through the park," she attempted. "All stone, with arches and Corinthian

17

columns. Did you have it built, Lady Raleigh, or is it old?"

"My husband's father had it built a quarter of a century ago."

"It's charming. Nigel tells me you have some paintings hung on tapestry in the gallery, in the old style."

"You wouldn't want to see that old rubbish," Nigel told her. "I say, Fleur, can I get you a glass of wine?"

"Tea will be arriving shortly," Lady Raleigh announced. She noticed Nigel hadn't offered Pamela wine. In fact, he had scarcely glanced at her. He was besotted with this wretched actress.

"Tea, so English." The marquise smiled politely, as her eyes slid hopefully to the wine table.

"You might want to attend the assembly in Hatfield this evening," Nigel continued, tempting the jaded lady with his simple country treats. "Are you planning to attend, Mama?"

"We will be taking you and Pamela," his mother replied.

"By Jove, you'll like that, Fleur. What a stir you'll cause amongst all the local bucks."

Lord Breslau had thawed out sufficiently to leave the grate. "Were you just offering sherry, Nigel? I'll have one, if you please."

"Tea is on the way," Lady Raleigh repeated. "You may have wine if you prefer, Breslau. How is your mama?"

"I must confess I have no idea. She doesn't write—letters, I mean. My housekeeper would have notified me if she were ill or dead, however, so I expect she is fine."

18

Lady Raleigh gave him a pained look. "You haven't written in weeks, Nigel," was her next attempt at conversation.

"How can you say so, Mama? Didn't I write just last week and tell you Fleur was coming for a visit?"

"And the very next day to add that I, too, was coming," Breslau pointed out. "Why, you've been deluged with letters, madam. Mama would box my ears if I bombarded her with so many epistles."

Pamela stared at Lord Breslau as though he were an exotic animal in a zoo. She had never heard such strange conversation in her life, the voice and manner so polite, and the words so offensive. She hardly knew what tone to take toward him. In her experience, gentlemen came in two categories. There were the eligible ones, who were given the encouragement of smiles for any attempt at conversation, and there was the other sort. Despite his title, his fortune, and his fame, Breslau clearly fell into the latter category. She exchanged a bewildered look with Lady Raleigh.

Her hostess was saved the exertion of being polite in the face of such levity by the arrival of the tea tray. "You may pour, Pamela," she said, to show the actress who had pride of place in her saloon.

"Do you get to the theater very often, Mees Calmstock?" the marquise asked.

"Pamela doesn't attend the theater. She was very well raised," Lady Raleigh replied, and passed a plate of biscuits to the actress.

The marquise accepted one with a gracious smile. She turned her head to Breslau and winked, covering her smile with a biscuit.

"Oh, I say, Mama!" Nigel objected. "Everyone attends the theater. It's not like the old days."

Pamela gave a conspiratorial smile in the general direction of the marquise. "I should love to see you perform sometime, madam—onstage, I mean," she said daringly.

"I shall send you tickets for my debut in tragedy," the marquise promised, with a long look at Breslau, whose interest had wandered to Miss Comstock. Was it possible there was a spark of wit in Nigel's little lump?

"Well now, that should satisfy you, Lady Raleigh," he said. "Miss Comstock will have a long wait to attend the theater if that is to be her first visit. Your next play is to be Crowell's comedy, *The Amazing Invalid,* Fleur, as you very well know. He's a new writer of great talent."

"I think not, Wes," Lady Chamaude replied, and accepted a cup of tea. "When you, who haven't approved of any writer since *Beowulf* was written, start praising an unknown, I know what you are about. You have found a silly farce for me. My next performance will be a tragedy. I have quite made up my mind."

Lady Raleigh's nostrils tightened to see the actress on such intimate terms with Breslau. Breslau's name was Westbrook Hume, but even his close friends called him Breslau. It was only family who were allowed the intimacy of Wes. She never used that nickname herself.

"But I bought the *Invalid* for you. It's a marvelous role," he exclaimed.

The marquise gave him a coy look. "I hear they're

trying to find someone to play Desdemona in *Othello* at the Garden."

"That's hardly a starring role for a lady. The Moor is the star."

"Desdemona gets to die, and that can be the making of a tragic actress," the marquise countered. "It's a story much to my liking. Secret marriage, schemes and intrigues, jealousy, and, of course, in the end the men make a great mess of it all, just like real life. A lady would have handled it more adroitly. We are much better at intrigue, don't you agree, Lady Raleigh?" she asked.

Lady Raleigh gave a snort of disgust. "It is precisely the sort of play I most despise. Why should I pay to watch the dissipation I avoid in my own live, and that of my family?"

The marquise gave her a glittering smile. "One might manage to free her own life of intrigue, if she has a taste for dullness, but how, pray, do you keep it from your family? Perhaps I should pose that question to the gentlemen," she said, and cast a sly glance at Sir Aubrey.

He frowned and said evasively, "Some plays are well enough. I prefer a comedy myself."

"Sheridan, the playwright—so clever—says tragedy is just comedy with the characters dying in the end instead of getting married." Her infamous eyes flickered swiftly from Sir Aubrey to his dame. "Even marriage, I daresay, is not necessarily a guarantee of a happy ending."

Pamela bit back a smile. Her hostess was silently fuming. Sir Aubrey looked as if he had swallowed a hot coal, and Nigel was fidgeting uncomfortably.

21

Only Lord Breslau appeared immune to the undercurrents at work in the room.

"But on the stage," he said to the marquise, "we allow our disbelief to hang suspended and pretend all will be well. In any case, even a bad marriage leaves more hope than a set of corpses."

The marquise considered this a moment. "Perhaps you are right, Wes. It's true that husbands and wives seem unwilling to leave a marriage, however unhappy it is. They will go to great lengths to preserve the form, when the content is gone."

Sir Aubrey was subjected to another penetrating shot from the marquise, and stirred restively in his chair. Lady Raleigh found the conversation not only unsavory but pointless. She was aware of her butler hovering beyond the doorway, which was a clue he wished to speak to her.

"Excuse me," she said. "I must speak to Wetmore."

"The butler," Nigel explained to Lady Chamaude. "That would be about your wanting the downstairs bedchamber. The marquise always likes to sleep downstairs when she can," he explained to the others. "Since we have a guest suite downstairs, I told her she might have it."

"It is a foolish habit left over from the terror in France," the lady said. "My dear husband was pulled from his bed in the dead of night and taken to the Bastille. I always felt if we had been sleeping downstairs we would have heard them come, and perhaps Henri might have escaped. To this day I still feel unsafe in an upstairs bedchamber. The past has a way of hanging about us," she said sadly, just before

22

she fixed Sir Aubrey with another of those peculiarly meaningful looks.

"You needn't fear for your life at Belmont," Nigel said heartily, and moved down to the end of the sofa to be closer to the marquise.

"I know it is foolishness on my part," she agreed. "We actresses are a superstitious lot. I surround myself with good-luck charms. This shawl," she said, holding up the elegant paisley garment, "is my good-luck piece. I never travel without it."

The gentlemen smiled fondly at this evidence of ignorant superstition. Pamela regarded the shawl and noticed it looked remarkably new for a shawl that had done much traveling. The threads of the long silk fringe each hung separately. They would have bunched into unsightly clumps if the shawl were old. Its color, too, in shades of green and rose, matched the lady's suit superbly, but would look quite at odds with other colors. An affectation, Pamela decided, and ascribed it to the marquise's love of drama.

When Lady Chamaude wrapped the shawl over her shoulders, Nigel sprang up from the sofa to help her. "*Merci, chéri*," she murmured with a soft glance. Pamela was extremely glad Lady Raleigh wasn't there to see that look.

"I shall wear my good-luck charm when I go to the Garden to discuss playing Desdemona," the marquise continued, directing her words to Breslau now. "I hear they are paying their leading ladies fifty pounds per performance. That was what Siddons made, at any rate."

"We'll discuss your salary at another time, Fleur,"

he replied. "In any case, tragedy pays no more than comedy, if that is what you are implying."

"A lady has to think of her future, when she has grown too old to perform."

Sir Aubrey waited for her head to turn in his direction. On this occasion he was spared, but he knew in his bones the words were uttered for his benefit. She had come to hold him to ransom.

"Pardon me," he said, and rose from his seat. "I see Dot is beckoning me from the hall."

A short silence fell over the remaining company. "More tea, anyone?" Pamela asked.

Breslau strolled languidly toward the tea tray and held out his cup.

## Chapter Three

"Well, Miss Comstock," Breslau said, with that heartiness reserved for invalids, poor relations, unattractive lumps of girls, and other social misfits, "I was happy to hear you are not averse to the theater."

Pamela carefully filled his cup, and when she handed it to him, he noticed the lump had rather pretty eyes. They reminded him of his favorite cat's eyes—a tawny topaz shade, wide-spaced in her pale face. Her nose, too, had a kittenish touch to it that set ill with his preconceptions of Miss Comstock.

"I don't get many opportunities to attend, but I adore it."

Breslau hesitated between a meaningless condolence and a joke. "That shows a lack of initiative on your part," he said, opting for the latter.

She knew by this time that his conversation was unusual, and showed no surprise. "Does it? I thought it only betrayed my rustic abode. We don't get many traveling players in the country."

"This is true," he nodded, assessing her quite openly.

"To show you we are not completely out of it, however, I can assure you I attended the theater just last week. Tuck's Traveling Players gave us an excellent performance of *The Beggar's Opera.*"

Breslau stood holding his cup, undecided where to sit. He now took up a seat beside Pamela. "If you endured the entire performance, you are indeed an irreclaimable lover of the theater."

"Have you actually heard of Tuck's?"

"Worse, I've seen them perform, but with the excuse that it was in the line of duty. I cull performers from the traveling groups. Tuck's has never yielded anything resembling the Flawless Fleur."

"She's wonderful, isn't she? I never could understand the story of Helen of Troy till I saw her."

"Fleur's an intriguing cross between Helen of Troy and Lucrezia Borgia," he said, with the unworthy aim of shocking her. She only looked confused. "You really ought to bestir yourself to attend the London Season."

"If I had the sort of initiative you're recommending I'd move to London, but my parents are so unimaginative. Papa feels he must be home to look after the farm. Sugar, cream?"

"Just sugar, please." Breslau didn't continue immediately. His eyes lingered over Miss Comstock's lively face. The chit was no Incomparable, but she had a certain charm. He always preferred conversation to less animate pulchritude. "Nigel often speaks of you," he said. What Nigel had failed to mention was that his intended was not in the first blush of youth. For himself, Breslau preferred a little maturity.

26

"You have already warned me. What does he say?" she asked bluntly.

Expecting some token of pleasure, Breslau was thrown for a loss by her question. "All manner of compliments. I shan't repeat them, or—"

"Afraid I'll dash this hot tea in your face?" she said, and smiled at his discomfiture. That had removed his haughty expression. "Never mind, Lord Breslau. The only thing he might have said in my favor is that I have ten thousand pounds, and am his mama's goddaughter."

"I shan't repeat them, or your head will swell," he continued, as though she hadn't interrupted. Breslau examined her with disconcerting frankness, and noticed her head would have a hard time growing, confined as it was by that hair, all skinned into a bun. That gamine little face was crying out for curls. She was still young enough to make a charming ingenue.

Miss Comstock lifted her cup and sipped daintily. "It's going to be a lovely weekend, don't you think?" she said, setting her cup down.

He glanced toward the window, where a sullen and sunless sky bathed the landscape in gloom. "Are you speaking of the weather?"

"Hardly! I refer to the company."

"You have bizarre taste, Miss Comstock. Like the weather, the party threatens to be stormy."

"That's exactly what I mean! Something exciting will happen, at last." She lowered her voice. "You can't imagine how boring these visits usually are. I had no idea the Flawless Fleur would be here."

"And here I dared to imagine *my* presence added something to the pending excitement."

She considered this a moment. "I shouldn't think so. Actually your presence detracts from the intrigue, but I'm sure Lady Chamaude will enjoy your company excessively. Nigel won't have her all to himself."

"Nigel?" he asked, surprised.

"Oh, *you* thought of that, too. No, Sir Aubrey wouldn't dare tackle her when his wife is on guard."

Breslau felt a pronounced urge to exclaim, Miss Comstock! in the outraged accents of his spinster aunts. Then he saw the gleam of laughter in her topaz eyes, and feared he was going to speak as one shouldn't to an innocent country lass.

"How old are you?" he asked instead.

"Twenty-two. What has that got to do with anything?"

"The parents are slow in bringing this match between you and Nigel to fruition."

"Not really. Nigel is only twenty-two as well. It's pretty ancient for a lady, of course, but the pragmatics of matchmaking decree that a gentleman of two and twenty is scarcely breeched. I expect we can stave them off for two more years, and by then I hope to have—" She stopped and bit her lip. Why was she rattling on so freely to this stranger?

"Found someone more to your liking?" he suggested.

"I've seen enough of marriage; I'm not eager to incarcerate myself. At twenty-four, I come in charge of my dowry. It was left to me by an aunt, and Papa can't keep it from me."

"Will it be a farm in the country, like the ladies of Llangollen?"

"Certainly not! I've had enough of that. I want to

28

broaden myself in London. The theater, balls, the shops."

"An intellectual," he nodded. "Will you be setting up a bluestocking saloon?"

"I don't own any blue stockings. Never mind smirking, Lord Breslau. I know what a bluestocking is," she added sharply. "I have no intellectual pretentions. No, what I should like to do is live with my older brother, Harley. He's an M.P., you must know."

"I didn't. Nigel failed to relate that in your favor. Would his wife condone such a *ménage à trois*?"

"He doesn't have one at the moment, though two recent letters have mentioned a Miss Greenwood in such casual terms that I'm considerably concerned. In any case, I could always have my own apartment in their house, for I wouldn't like to live all alone, with only some wretched spinster relative to keep me company."

"You know, of course, what happens to young ladies who don't nab a *parti*? They eventually grow into that dread species, the spinster relative, themselves."

Pamela's attention strayed to Nigel and the marquise. He was gazing into her eyes, besotted. "Would you mind rescuing him, Lord Breslau, before Lady Raleigh returns and catches him making a cake of himself?"

Breslau took up his cup. "With the greatest reluctance, Miss Comstock." A quick frown of incomprehension flashed across her mobile face. "That was a compliment. I am fond of Fleur's company."

"Oh, but you prefer mine! How flattering!"

Breslau inclined his head to hers. A glint of amusement removed the edge of cynicism from his aristocratic features. "If you and your ten thousand pounds have any notion of taking London by storm when you move in with Harley, I might just drop you a hint. Young ladies aren't required to utter every thought that crops into their pates. A simple blush of pleasure would have been more appropriate."

"I shall bear that in mind, in the unlikely case that any other gentleman is kind enough to pretend he prefers my company to that of the marquise's."

"Young gentlemen, too, are sometimes required to restrain their tongues. Mum's the word on that charge of pretending. Why do you suppose we bother pretending to young ladies?" he asked with a lazy smile. This was flattery of a high order in Breslau's opinion. It merited, and in any saloon in London would have earned, a simper of delight. Why did it cause Miss Comstock to frown, and stare at him so oddly.

Good gracious, he's trying to *flirt* with me! I must set him down at once. "In Chatham, it usually presages a flirtation, but no doubt in London they have some less innocent intention. Which I, of course, shan't mention after your kind hint. I must have Lady Chamaude teach me to blush."

"You *are* blushing, Miss Comstock. Well, well. And here I thought Nigel was exaggerating when he called you—"A light laugh lifted his thin lips. "More unutterable phrases."

Her eyes darted over his shoulder, quite ignoring the advances of the most sought-after parti in London. "Lord Breslau, hurry! He's holding her hand. His mother will kill him!"

Breslau cast a fairly disinterested eye toward the sofa. "Surely she'll reserve slaughter for the engagement. Holding hands merits no more than a hundred lashes."

"Aren't you even a little jealous?"

"Of whom?"

"Nigel and the Flawless One, of course."

"No, only of Nigel," he said, and finally rose to insert himself between Nigel and the marquise, leaving Miss Comstock to sip tea with a pensive gleam in her eye.

She heard the muted hush of angry voices in the hallway, and wandered closer to try to make out the words.

Lady Raleigh was laying down the law in no uncertain terms. "The downstairs bedchamber, you see. The hussy plans to entertain Nigel after we are all abed."

"Rubbish," Sir Aubrey said. "Let her sleep downstairs. We don't want her any closer to the rest of us than she must be."

His wife approved of this un-Christian sentiment, but still Nigel's virtue took precedence. "I have half a mind to lock his door and remove the key after he retires."

"He'd only crawl out the window, if *that* is what they're up to."

Lady Raleigh was silent a moment while her mind canvased other options. "We've put Breslau in the Tudor suite. Nigel can sleep in the spare cot in his dressing room."

"If Breslau sleeps in his own bed."

His wife was happy to see Aubrey was alive to all the sinful possibilities inherent in the situation. "If he's with the actress, then Nigel is safe," she pointed out.

31

"It will look odd, billeting him on Breslau."

"I'll throw some dustcovers over Nigel's bed and open a bottle of turpentine. I'll say the room's being painted."

"What of the other guest rooms?"

"Not aired, and very drafty. With Nigel's weak chest, he must have a warm room. I'll speak to the housekeeper about it at once."

"That'll do then," Sir Aubrey decided. "I'm retiring to my study till dinner. I can't abide that woman's vulgar chatter."

His good wife could hardly believe her ears. It almost seemed her prayers were answered, and Aubrey had given up his shameless ways. To voluntarily remove himself from an actress when his wife wasn't even in the room was an unprecedented thing. She hastened off to consult with the housekeeper, and Sir Aubrey went to his office, trembling.

How much would Corinne demand? He wasn't a wealthy man. A thousand pounds would strap him pretty badly. He was sitting with his head in his hands when he heard a light tap at the door. Dot and the servants didn't bother to knock. It must be Breslau. Was he aware of what was going on? He was a man-about-town at least—he might know what Lord Alban was soaked for.

He hurried to the door. "Sir Aubrey, I find you alone, just as I hoped," the marquise said, and sauntered in, hips swaying just as he remembered. "You and I shall have a little talk, *hein?* About the olden days, in Brighton. Perhaps we should close the door?" she suggested with an arch look.

In the saloon, Breslau watched the marquise leave, and was at a loss as to why she should be running after Sir Aubrey. What had she meant by all that talk of Brighton? Breslau was familiar with all Fleur's moods and expressions. The mood she took to Sir Aubrey's office was one that presaged no good.

It suddenly occurred to Nigel that he hadn't exchanged a single sentence with Pamela since arriving. "I wonder what Fleur wants to talk to Papa about," he said.

"Probably the old days at Brighton. Is her book full of scandal, Nigel?"

"Certainly not! It isn't that sort of thing at all. Just because Fleur is an actress, it don't mean she has loose morals, you know. She's a regular martyr if you want the truth. A heroine. You've no idea what that woman's been through."

"About two dozen lovers, according to gossip," Pamela suggested before she got a rein on her tongue.

Breslau listened silently as he went to the side table to exchange his teacup for a glass of wine.

"She has not," Nigel said like a sulky boy. "It's just her generous nature that misleads folks. There are going to be a lot of surprised people if they think her memoirs are scandalous."

"A lot of disappointed people," Pamela added.

During a short silence, they all heard the sound of raised voices coming from the study. Pamela's eyes lit up with interest. She noticed that Breslau didn't return to the group, but hovered close to the door, where he might hope to catch the odd word from the study.

She ran to the table, grabbed a glass of wine, and joined him. The draft from the front door sent a

33

shiver up her bare arms. "It's nice and cool here," she said. "So stuffy by the fire."

"Goose bumps become you, Miss Comstock."

"Shh!" she exclaimed shamelessly, and tilted her head toward the study. "What did she say? Did you catch that?"

"It sounded like 'your son.' You don't suppose Aubrey charged her with corrupting a minor?"

"Brighton—it sounded like Brighton."

"Shall we put a glass to the door?" Breslau asked, and smiled.

"There!" Pamela said, her eyes glistening with excitement. "She said 'your son,' again. Doesn't she sound angry? I wish Sir Aubrey would speak louder. I can't make out a word he says."

"He was always a contrary gent."

Pamela sidled into the hall, ostensibly to look at a Chinese planter holding a fatigued palm tree, but with one ear turned to the door. Breslau peered toward the staircase, then down the other way, and looked a question at her.

"Something about quarter day," she whispered.

"What the deuce are you two doing?" Nigel called in a querulous voice, and joined them.

"We were just admiring the palm," Pamela said, and quickly returned to the saloon with him.

Nigel cast a certain look at Breslau, as though to say, What did I tell you? As dull as ditch water.

That look called Pamela back to her role as dullard. "Mama has a very nice palm in the reading room at home," she said. "Did I tell you, Nigel, your mother gave me one of Hanna More's tracts for the reformation of the poor for Christmas? She recom-

34

mends I join the Religious Tract Society. It sounds very interesting."

"What do they do?" Nigel asked.

"Why, they reform the poor and write tracts about it I suppose," she replied vaguely."

Breslau stared at Miss Comstock, wondering if he had been misled by the woman who had sat with him at the tea tray a moment ago. Had he mistaken country manners for wit?

"Hanna would do better to reform the rich," he said.

Miss Comstock lifted an innocent eye and replied, "The rich, I fear, are past reclaiming."

"What are you calling rich, madam? Anything over, say, ten thousand pounds?"

Pamela failed to catch the reference to her dowry. "Ten thousand per annum isn't rich. It's obscene," she replied.

"I didn't mean per annum. And I hope I am not obscene."

She inhaled sharply. No one had ten thousand a year. "Do you have that much, Breslau? What on earth do you do with so much money?" Nigel gave a sound of disgust and she quickly added, "Did you ever consider joining the Religious Tract Society, milord? What a lot of tracts we could publish with your blunt."

"This is true, but I find better things to do with my blunt than chastize the poor for not being rich."

It was his odd manner of speech rather than his answer that caught her interest. She had observed it twice now. "Why do you say 'this,' when you mean 'that'?"

Before Breslau could answer, Sir Aubrey's office

door suddenly opened and the sound of polite laughter echoed in the hall. Pamela shot Breslau a curious glance.

"I'll leave you two a moment's privacy," he said. "I have a few matters to discuss with Fleur."

Miss Comstock's eyes had lost their kittenish look. An angry hue suffused her cheeks. Nigel might be against this match; his opposition was nothing to Miss Comstock's. She dreaded as much as a moment alone with her reluctant suitor. Breslau would like to have stayed for her performance of a prude, for he had decided that was what accounted for her sudden change in manner, but if Fleur was up to something, he wanted to know and put a stop to it.

A self-promoting autobiography was all well and good. It might heat up interest in his leading lady, but he didn't want her blackmailing her former patrons. That stunt would empty the theater, if word got around. Her raised voice had sounded quite angry. It wasn't like Fleur to be so obtuse. She had recently developed a bourgeois mania for respectability. He assumed her persistence in getting herself invited to Belmont had been a step toward making herself respectable.

Sir Aubrey's study door was closing when Breslau reached the hallway. Fleur was just snapping the clasp on her reticule and smiling contentedly. Breslau stared a moment at the reticule, then lifted his icy eyes to his leading lady.

Fleur was not unduly perturbed by that look, but she was swift to speak of other things. "I hoped Sir Aubrey might recall a few anecdotes for my memoirs, but I drew a blank. What a gothic old heap this place is. I daresay they water the wine. I could use a glass of brandy."

"You won't find any here, but the wine is excellent. You haven't done something foolish, have you, Fleur?"

The marquise assumed her most innocent pose, eyes wide open and guileless, a pucker of her brow indicating confusion. "What do you mean, Wes?"

"It sounded as if you and Sir Aubrey were arguing."

"Not at all. I scolded him a little for his bad memory, but we patched it up in the end."

"He is on excellent terms with Max, you must know," Breslau cautioned.

"Why do you think I'm here?" she asked, and laughed. "General Maxwell mentioned he would be attending the winter assembly at Hatfield."

"Does Max know you're here?"

"I hinted I would be visiting Belmont. He didn't believe me. *Now* he'll see I'm accepted in respectable homes."

"So that's it!" Breslau said, and nodded. "You hope to get an offer from him."

It was common knowledge in theatrical circles that General Maxwell was pursuing the Flawless Fleur. No one, including Breslau, knew what degree of success he had had, but Fleur was still residing in her own apartment, and paying her own rent. Max certainly didn't have marriage in mind, but apparently Fleur was holding out for a golden ring.

A prim and proper lady wouldn't do for a gent like General Max, who had spent his youth racketing around from war to war. The chief obstacle was the general's mother. Mrs. Maxwell was a friend of Lady

Raleigh's, and of similar piosity. As she had a large fortune and two daughters, there was plenty of competition for the fortune.

"I don't plan to grow old and fat and gray on the public stage, like Mrs. Siddons," Fleur replied. "When I am past it, I shall marry and become a Mrs. Grundy. Max is the likeliest prospect at the moment. You must stand up with me at the assembly this evening, Wes, and present the loftiest lords at the ball to me. Max doesn't care a groat for such things, but I must impress the old Tartar."

"This is not the point at which our interests touch, Fleur," he said, but in a bantering way. "I'm in no hurry to lose my leading lady."

"Oh, I don't plan to retire for three years. I have every intention of performing in a few *tragedies* first," she said, and placed her hand on his arm.

"Make it a few comedies, and I might be coerced into helping you."

"You know how to put me in an agreeable mood," she teased, and began walking down the hall with him. "Greed is the last infirmity of noble minds, according to your Shakespeare."

"Actually it was Milton, and fame is the spur, not greed."

"Pedant!"

Pamela watched them from the saloon. She felt a little stab of annoyance when the Flawless Fleur reached up and wagged Breslau's chin. Such a familiar gesture betrayed close intimacy. Nigel followed her gaze and his eyes blazed with jealousy. He was on his feet in an instant, pelting toward them.

"Sonny." The marquise smiled fondly and put her hand on his arm. This motion stirred no emotion but a mild surprise in Pamela's bosom. "Be a darling and show me to my room. You know Maria, my dresser, was unable to accompany me because of her wretched cold. I must prepare my own toilette. And really I'm aching with fatigue."

"I'll call a servant to help you," Nigel said at once.

"I wouldn't dream of it. I'll run along now and rest before the ball this evening. What hour does your dear mama serve dinner?"

"Usually at six, but with company here she's putting it off till seven."

"Not on my account, I hope! I wouldn't want her to change her routine for me. Pray, tell her to consider me as family."

"Wes don't like country hours," he said.

Pamela wanted to hear the conversation. She noticed the marquise had left her favorite shawl on the sofa and took it up as an excuse to join them.

"Thank you, Mees Calmstock." The marquise smiled. "I should have worn this to your papa's study, Nigel, and he wouldn't have lost his temper with me."

Nigel blanched. "What did he say to you? You didn't tell him—" He came to a red-faced, guilty halt, and looked at Pamela, who was regarding him suspiciously.

The marquise said archly, "Ask Wes. He was listening at the door, I think." Then she turned and made her exit. Nigel went with her to point out the way.

The remainder of her audience watched her undulate gracefully away, toward the guest suite at the end of the hall. Nigel soon came hurrying back.

"What did Papa say to her, Wes?" he asked.

"Nothing to worry about. They parted on excellent terms."

"More importantly, what is it you fear she might have told him?" Pamela demanded.

"It's none of your business," he retorted before turning back to Breslau. "Did you hear anything?"

"I'm not a dog. My ears have only human capacity. I heard raised voices, that's all."

"I knew this visit would be a disaster," Nigel moaned. "I thought Papa at least would like Fleur. I was sure it'd be Mama who squelched her."

"Then why did you invite her?" Pamela asked.

"I didn't! That is, well . . . it's hard getting a moment to go over the memoirs in the city. Wes gave her two nights off from the theater and she kept pestering me to come here. It had to be done sooner or later," he added grimly.

"Why?" Pamela demanded. The awful idea was beginning to take hold that Nigel had offered for the marquise.

"You'll know when the time comes. Just remember I never asked you to marry me. It was all Mama's idea."

This was as good as a confirmation. "Nigel, you idiot!"

"She hasn't said yes," he admitted. "I wonder if I should ask her again now?"

"This is hardly the optimum moment. She's aching with fatigue," Breslau reminded him. He had no fear that Fleur had raised this ridiculous matter with Nigel's father.

"Then I suppose I might as well entertain you," Nigel said to Pamela with an amazing lack of enthusiasm. "It will put Mama in a good mood. Would you like to play fiddlesticks or something?"

"No, I'd like to beat you with a mallet. I can't believe you actually proposed to the marquise. She's old enough to be your mother."

Breslau saw no jealousy in her behavior, only the frustration of a sane adult for the folly of youth.

"Lots of men marry older ladies."

"You're not a man. You're a stupid boy."

"Fleur don't think so! And what you really mean is that Fleur ain't a lady."

"No more she is!"

On this rejoinder, Nigel strutted into the saloon and went to the cupboard where the games were kept. "Well, do you want to play fiddlesticks or not?" he asked brusquely.

"No, that's childish."

"You don't know how to play chess."

"Neither do you."

"I beat you last time at least."

"That was checkers."

Breslau listened, with a mocking smile tugging at his lips. "Do you have any puppets in the house? Punch and Judy suggests itself as a suitable game for you feuding young lovers."

"We must talk," Pamela said. "You can't have mentioned this to your parents yet, Nigel, or they'd be in the boughs."

"I'll tell them when the time comes, and meanwhile I don't want you running to Mama."

"I shan't embarrass you, for there isn't a chance in the world the marquise would have you. What do you think, Breslau?" she asked.

"I think we should all play fiddlesticks."

41

When Lady Raleigh returned, she found the three of them at this childish pastime, and was happy she had an excuse to remove Breslau. She beckoned him to the hallway and spoke in low tones.

"Sorry to inconvenience you, Breslau, but I have a small favor to ask. Would you mind terribly if Nigel used the cot in your dressing room tonight? His bedroom is being redone."

She went on with her highly unlikely tale. Breslau listened impassively and expressed every pleasure at the annoyance of having a puppy snoring in the next room. He wanted his duties to be quite clear and asked bluntly, "You want me to keep an eye on him, I take it?"

"Oh, no indeed! It is just that—why did she insist on having the downstairs suite? That looks a trifle odd you must own."

It was true that Fleur had never expressed this fear of an upstairs bedchamber before. Her apartment in London, in fact, was on the second story. He didn't believe she was after Nigel in a romantic way, though Fleur was known to have a filly's tooth where young gentlemen were concerned. If Maxwell should publicly spurn her at the assembly, there was no saying what her temper might lead her to do.

"Why don't we slip a draught of laudanum into his wine after the assembly?" he suggested.

"I never have it in the house. I disapprove of laudanum. Oh, and there is one more thing, Breslau. I would prefer if *you* would ask Nigel to share your suite. He wouldn't question it, coming from you. He'll insist on using one of the vacant guest suites if I suggest it. And with his lungs, you know . . ."

"What reason could I possibly give?"

"You got him this assignment editing the actress's memoirs." A note of accusation crept into her voice. "Perhaps you can make up some new job you wish to discuss with him."

"I don't know any other actors who are writing their memoirs."

"He writes as well as edits. Ask him to write you a play for Drury Lane. He would be flattered."

Breslau's eyes widened in amazement. "Well he might be!"

You will think of something," Lady Raleigh assured him, and went off to attend to other hostessing chores.

She went tapping at the marquise's door to see if she required anything. The woman didn't answer. She hadn't brought a maid or dresser with her, as a lady should. That meant she'd be requisitioning one of the servants for her dressing. At least the wretched woman was sleeping. Her sort was probably up half the night, and slept the daylight away.

There was no denying the actress was pretty, though, in her own garish way. She'd take the shine out of the ladies at the assembly. Some vestigial atom of feminine competitiveness urged Lady Raleigh to enliven her own evening toilette. Her usual outfit for winter do's was a well-aged blue silk gown. There wasn't time to have a new gown constructed, but she would wear the Raleigh diamonds. The local assembly generally merited no more than her pearls.

When she went after Aubrey to get the diamonds out of the family safe, she found him in his study, going over his account books.

"You always wear the pearls," he reminded her.

"Usually, but tonight I shall wear the family heirlooms."

"They're not family heirlooms. Not entailed," Sir Aubrey pointed out brusquely.

"They were passed down from your mama, and Pamela shall wear them when she marries Nigel. They are family heirlooms, whether they are entailed or not."

"Wear your pearls," Aubrey said. "I don't see why you must ape the manners of an actress."

Lady Raleigh was much impressed by this streak of common sense from her lord and master. "You're quite right, Aubrey. There is some insidious evil in having a woman like that under the roof. I was being drawn into the snare without realizing it. I shall read a few chapters from my Bible before dinner. And by the by, I arranged to have Breslau keep an eye on Nigel. He'll not be visiting that harpy downstairs, and neither shall Breslau," she added contentedly.

She was happy to see how this pleased her husband. Shows of affection had been rare nearly to the point of nonexistence between them for a decade, but she placed her hand on his now and squeezed gently. Aubrey returned the pressure. She would leave the door between their adjoining bedrooms open tonight. A man had his needs, and it was best to fill them when an evil woman was amongst them, however unpleasant it might be. Lady Raleigh spared no exertion in her quest for salvation for her and hers.

"I keep the pearls in my jewelry box, so I shan't bother you any longer." She glanced at his account books, and at the frown that furrowed his brow. "We haven't outrun the grocer, have we, Aubrey?"

"No, no, but I shall put off mending the stalls till the spring. I like to keep a little beforehand with the world."

In Lady Raleigh's opinion, the stables ate up more than their share of the family income. "That might be best." She smiled, and finally left.

The Lord did indeed work in strange ways, His wonders to perform. Who would have thought a visit from an actress would open up Aubrey's eyes to the folly of human vanity? Perhaps Nigel's work with the creature would bring him to a proper appreciation of Pamela. He would be better served if he had a good wife with him in wicked London. Twenty-two was old enough for a man to marry. And poor Pamela must be growing impatient.

## Chapter Four

Pamela Comstock stood at the mirror examining her hair. At home, the upstairs maid did it for her. She didn't have a personal maid, or want one. Neither did she want one of Lady Raleigh's servants twisting her curls into some style of yesteryear. Her hair was her crowning glory. A rich mane of chestnut waves tumbled to her shoulders and gleamed in the lamplight. She always wore it tightly pinned in Nigel's presence, but on this visit she would risk wearing it in a more becoming style. Nigel would be fully occupied with Fleur, and there was no reason the other gentlemen at the assembly should take her for a dowd.

Her mind roamed to Breslau, and she regretted once more not having brought her new rose gown with her. She was far from considering him a possible husband, but an eligible gentleman who honors a lady with a flirtation merits a good gown, especially when he is accustomed to London toilettes.

She tilted her head this way and that, assessing her face. Her eyes were all right. Her mouth was too small and her cheeks were pale. She pinched her cheeks till they burned, and stretched her lips in an O, an exercise vigorously followed, but one that showed no results. This done, she took up the brush and softened the waves over her forehead, allowing a few tendrils to tumble along her cheek. The rest of her hair was loosely pulled back in a basket with blue ribbons to match her gown.

Her simple toilette done, she opened the door and hurried along the hallway, past Lady Raleigh and Sir Aubrey's suite. The door was closed, but Nigel's piping voice carried through the door quite audibly. His stuttering, apologetic syllables suggested he had confessed his hope of marrying Fleur.

". . . not to say it is settled, you know, but I thought I should just drop you a hint."

"Have you spoken to your father?" Lady Raleigh's voice was as stiff and tough as a whip.

"I thought *you* might . . ."

"I never want to hear another word of this, Nigel. We shall forget you had the ill manners to speak to your mother about marrying an actress. I'd rather see you dead." She sounded as though she meant it literally.

Pamela heard footsteps approaching the door and darted back to her own room, as it was closer than the stairway. She remained there a moment, regretting Nigel's rashness. Not that she could entirely blame him. Working with Fleur must be a terrible temptation. The editing of the memoirs would now come to a halt. Lady Raleigh would see to that. Dinner promised to be extraordinarily uncomfortable.

When Pamela went downstairs, all the party except the marquise had assembled in the saloon. Lady Raleigh looked as stiff as an Egyptian mummy.

Other than that and a certain pallor, she revealed no sign of her agitation. Nigel, of course, was sulking.

"Pamela, my dear, you should have asked for a servant to help with your toilette," Lady Raleigh said. "Your hair is all falling down. You must stick a pin in it, or you'll look a quiz at the assembly." It pained the dame to see Pamela falling into the snare of competing with the actress, but she could not be hard on her. Had she not herself been tempted?

Nigel gave Pam a dismissing look. "Nobody will notice. What the deuce can be keeping Fleur?" He drew out his watch and *tsk'd* at it. Lady Raleigh's jaws clenched, but that was the only betrayal of her mood.

Pamela felt as though the room were resting on one of Mr. Goldsmith's rockets, and that it might go off at any moment and blow them all sky high. Fleur's dashing entrance at that moment occupied the others, and Breslau stole the opportunity to show Pamela a seat beside him.

"Don't frown, Miss Comstock," he said. "I think your hair looks charming."

She ignored the compliment. "He told Lady Raleigh," she said in a low voice. "Can't you do something to divert disaster?"

Breslau's face froze. "Who told her? Sir Aubrey?"

"No, Nigel. He wouldn't dare tell his father. He told his mother he plans to marry Fleur." Why this awful information should be a relief to Breslau was a mystery, but certainly the effect of it was to calm him noticeably. In fact, he even smiled. "What have I missed? What do you think Sir Aubrey might have told his wife? Has it to do with that argument in the library?" she asked.

Before he answered, Fleur was with them, and all attention centered on her. Pamela had been looking forward to a display of city dissipation, and didn't know whether she was relieved or disappointed at Fleur's gown. It was a pretty emerald green silk whose cut would have passed without comment at a meeting of the Religious Tract Society. The bodice was cut high, and the favorite paisley shawl covered her arms. The only item worth looking at was an impressive set of emeralds on her ears and at her neck. One might have added that the color of the actress's cheeks was unnaturally high, but that would have been mere quibbling. Fleur used a very light hand at the rouge pot. She looked respectable, but by no means a suitable bride for Nigel.

The marquise felt the chill in the air and braced herself to be fascinating. She was confident she could win over the coldest audience. "What a lovely rest I had," she said, smiling at her hostess, who appeared to be the source of the frost. "There is nothing like country quiet after the rigors of London. And what a charming suite you put me in, Lady Raleigh."

Lady Raleigh had been feeling generous, as Aubrey showed no appreciation of the guest, but her generosity had left her with Nigel's visit. Her breeding remained, and she said stiffly, "The wallpaper is from China."

"The chopsticks and fans suggested it might be," Fleur said, in accents that only Breslau recognized as gentle irony.

Sherry was served, and the little group began talking among themselves. Pamela leaned toward Breslau and said, "Well, this is a surprise I must say! I thought Lady Chamaude would wear a disgraceful gown. She dresses just like Mama."

He lifted a brow. "Then your mama is to be complimented."

"I just thought she would be more dashing."

"That would be because you aren't aware of the role Fleur's playing this evening. Country gentlewoman, I think, but don't fear it is Nigel she has her sites set on."

Pamela assumed it was Breslau himself who was Fleur's quarry. This struck her as being much closer to the mark. She noticed that a country gentlewoman did not empty her glass quite so quickly as Fleur, nor did she hold the empty glass out for a refill before her host suggested it. She kept these observations to herself. The idea was beginning to take hold that Breslau disliked any disparagement of his leading lady. One eyebrow had a way of rising to denote displeasure. He watched the marquise like a hawk, too, or like a man in love. Strange to think of Breslau being in love with anyone but himself.

Before long Lady Chamaude realized that any attention to Nigel went down ill, so she ignored him. Lady Raleigh was coolly polite, for she didn't want Aubrey to know what Nigel was up to. The meeting was extremely uncomfortable, but no uproar had broken out by the time dinner was announced. Fleur sat at Sir Aubrey's elbow, a little removed from his wife, which was a relief. At the end of the table, the hostess watched Fleur as though her guest planned to pocket the silverware. Over the meal, assiduous praise of the viandes brought a token glow of pleasure to Sir Aubrey's face.

"What delicious mutton," Lady Chamaude exclaimed. "I should love to taste your spring lamb." And a little sauce for this dry mutton!

"You knew it was our own," Sir Aubrey said with approval. "Most of the farmers hereabouts raise cattle, you must know. Very few of us are into sheep."

"Your son is constantly boasting about Belmont," the marquise told him.

Nigel was astonished to hear it. He would no more have discussed the farm with Fleur than he would discuss the greenroom with his mother. Fleur was certainly up to all the rigs. She just said that to turn Papa up sweet, and it was working, too, by Jove. The scowl he'd brought to the table had mellowed to civility when the ladies rose to leave. How did Fleur even know they raised sheep? You couldn't see them from the road.

When the ladies retired to the saloon, the gentlemen's taking of port was enlivened by Nigel's account of his extraordinary luck. "You'll never guess what, Papa. Wes has commissioned me to write a play for Drury Lane."

"Not commissioned!" Breslau objected swiftly. "I just suggested you think about it, after you've finished this editing job for Colchester."

Nigel had been so shocked to hear Breslau ask him to sleep in his suite that some excuse had to be given. Bereft of a sane one, Breslau had fallen back on Lady Raleigh's suggestion. "Sleep in the cot in my suite tonight, and we'll discuss it after the assembly."

"You would do better to come home and learn estate management," his father said.

"There's plenty of time for that. You are still young, Papa."

"How does it pay?" Sir Aubrey asked.

"That depends on how good it is," Nigel explained. "I'll get royalties every time it's performed, and if Colchester publishes it as a book, there'll be more money. It could run into thousands," he said blissfully.

"Of course not every play opens at Drury Lane or Covent Garden," Breslau threw in. "We might want to run it through the provinces for a few months till it's polished."

"What kind of a play did you have in mind?" his father asked. "Your mama won't want you writing anything risqué, lad."

"I wouldn't ask Fleur to perform anything licentious, Papa," Nigel said, offended.

A scowl alit on Sir Aubrey's brow. "*She's* to act it, is she?"

"Of course."

"The play hasn't been cast. The thing isn't even in the planning stage yet," Breslau said hastily. "It will give Nigel something to think about over the coming year."

"Year?" Nigel scoffed. "I'll have a finished manuscript on your desk within a month. I'm not one of those fellows who sweats and strains over every word. You'll see, Wes."

"Don't rush it. Take your time," Breslau urged.

During the next half hour, a dozen obscure plots were discussed. Sir Aubrey was nearly as relieved as Breslau to escape tales of sultans and pirates and wild Indians. They joined the ladies for the trip to the Hatfield assembly.

The marquise caused all the stir she was accustomed to when she entered the assembly hall on

Breslau's arm. Word had spread that she would be visiting Belmont, and the town awaited her arrival with bated breath. Like Miss Comstock, they expected a trifle more dash in her outfit, but overall they were thrilled. Several of them had seen her perform in London and came forward to tell her how much they enjoyed her work.

With Lady Raleigh at the helm, there was no question of Nigel being the actress's first partner. Breslau knew his duty, and he did it. He noticed Fleur's excitement when General Max entered the hall with his family. His mother and his two sisters and their husbands accompanied him. Max preceded the group with the same stately strut with which he preceded his men into battle. The general had long since abandoned his regimentals, but he still carried himself with a fine military air, and didn't object to being addressed as General Max.

The general had been an outstanding specimen of manhood in his youth. At fifty, he was still called handsome. His jet-black hair had thinned in front and silvered around the temples. It was true his jaw now more closely resembled jelly than concrete, but his eyes were still steely, and his nose as strong as ever. His shoulders had a harder time remaining erect with the beginning of a paunch to balance, but all in all he remained one of the sights of Hatfield.

All this aging virility had a way of feeling six years old when his mother fixed him with her own icy stare. "Hmph," she said. "I see Dot Raleigh has brought the actress along. We shan't recognize her. Dot has promised not to introduce us."

General Max hadn't owned up to knowing the marquise. It was his sisters who objected to this rough usage. "Oh, Mama! We can meet her. Everyone is. Look, there's Lord Breslau standing up with her, and he is top of the trees."

"Dot invited Breslau to keep the hussy from Aubrey. You ladies must consult with your husbands as to whether they will permit you to know the actress. Max and I shall visit the card room."

Max installed his mother at the whist table and darted back to the ballroom. It was going to be tricky knowing Fleur when Mama was in the card room, and cutting her when she was present. Mama was good for at least an hour at the card table, and he joined Breslau and Fleur as soon as the music ended.

Breslau breathed a sigh of relief and looked around for Pamela. "Miss Comstock?" he said, and offered her his arm.

She accepted it gratefully, thankful that her first session with Nigel was over. Her smile of relief told the story.

"It's best to get the unpleasant inevitable over with at the beginning. Then you can enjoy the rest of the evening," Breslau said.

"Why Lord Breslau," she exclaimed, frowning. "I don't in the least mind standing up with you. Where did you get such a notion?"

Breslau was speechless. He was accustomed to being courted, and felt he was doing Miss Comstock considerable honor by standing up with her. His stunned air gave Pamela pause.

Her hand flew to her mouth. "Oh," she said, aghast. "You meant Nigel!"

"I didn't realize I featured as an ogre in your mind."

"Of course not. No one is trying to make me marry

you. I should be happy to dance with you. Truly, I don't mind in the least."

"No further explanations are necessary, Miss Comstock," he said through thin lips. "Speaking of marriage, what had Nigel to say about his untimely confession to his mother?"

"I did most of the talking. I rang a good peel over him I can tell you. I told him his father would cut him off. That will make him think." After a frowning pause, she continued. "You never told me what it was you thought Sir Aubrey had told his wife. When we were speaking before dinner, some confusion arose. . . ."

"A misunderstanding. I assumed Nigel would discuss it with his father first." He looked around for a set to join.

Pamela frowned, dissatisfied with this explanation. Why should Breslau looked relieved when he learned the truth? But a ball wasn't the place to discuss it. To keep Fleur in good humor, it was to her set that Breslau led his partner. General Max's sisters, knowing their mama was safely bestowed behind a whist table, flew to join them, just a step behind their husbands. They were perfect pattern cards of smiling admiration. Fleur preened her feathers, and with a coy little smile at General Max, said, "Your sisters are even more charming than you told me."

This outrageous lie should have set the country bumpkins to smirking in pleasure. Fleur was hard put to account for the sudden stiffening of their faces.

Mrs. Stearne, the elder of the two, lifted a sapient brow and said to her brother, "Why, Max, you neglected to tell us you had the honor of the marquise's acquaintance before this evening."

The younger sister added mischievously, "Mama will be so thrilled. You must present the marquise to her. Perhaps we can all sit together for dinner."

Fleur was something of an expert at reading expressions and interpreting snubs. No sloth herself in delivering a setdown, she replied haughtily, "Unfortunately I have promised to dine with Lord Breslau. Perhaps another time, ladies."

General Max glared at the assembled company. He didn't know which one he'd like to run his sword through first. How dare Fleur announce their friendship in front of his family! How dare his sisters roast her in public. And worst of all, how dare Breslau try to cut him out!

The innocent chit with Breslau was the only one he could speak to without cursing, so he ignored Fleur's taunt and turned his fulminating stare on Pamela. "Visiting Belmont again, eh, Miss Comstock? I hope we shall soon have the permanent pleasure of your company amongst us."

His speech brought a frown to the last smiling face in the group, and in this awful mood, they began dancing.

"Do I detect undercurrents in our set?" Pam asked Breslau when the steps of the dance allowed them a moment's privacy.

"If you've detected the ill will, then it's no longer an undercurrent."

"Is she General Max's flirt?" Pam asked eagerly.

"Not when she is at Hatfield, it seems."

"Mrs. Maxwell wouldn't approve."

As soon as the dance was over, Maxwell's sisters

flew toward the card room. General Max knew he was in for it, and got rid of Fleur before his mother could come pouncing down on them. He left her standing alone, turned tail and ran without even thanking her for the dance. Fleur's nostrils quivered in mute fury. She retired from the floor with Breslau and Pamela.

Breslau tried to calm her. "Fleur, don't let this—"

"Save your directions for the stage, milord. This is my affair." She strode angrily off to the ladies cloakroom to recover her equanimity.

"Didn't I tell you it would be exciting!" Pamela exclaimed. Her topaz eyes were gleaming with the unwonted pleasure of the melodrama.

"You're in for even greater excitement before the night's over. Fleur won't take this sitting down."

"I wonder why she started all this brouhaha. I don't mean about Nigel—I acquit her of that. But if she's a close friend of General Max's, she must know how his mama would dislike the friendship."

"Fleur doesn't flinch from a little drama. Fur will fly before the night's over," Breslau replied. A frown pleated his brow as he watched her stormy exit.

"I had the impression at dinner that she was walking on eggs, and bending over backward not to upset the Raleighs."

A smile quirked Breslau's lip at this mixing of metaphors. "She was bound to crack a few shells, trying to walk on eggs in such an ungainly posture."

"You know what I mean."

They strolled to the refreshment parlor for a glass of ratafia, which inferior beverage was still popular in the provinces. Her recent encounters with drama

57

made Pamela realize how dreary her life was. For a brief moment she began visualizing herself in Fleur's shoes.

As Breslau led her to a seat she said, "It must be exciting, working in the theater. Producing plays is a game, really. I fancy anyone could do it."

"Fancy again. It's hard work."

"Of course, it's rather déclassé," she added pensively.

Once more Breslau's mobile brow rose to denote his disapproval. "Oh, I don't mean for you, Lord Breslau. How quick you are to take offense, like a deb of uncertain provenance. I was thinking of myself as an actress. It can't be infra dig for a gentleman to involve himself peripherally in the theater."

The sensitive eyebrow rose higher. Breslau considered himself more or less the focus of Drury Lane.

His companion ignored these subtle signs of dissatisfaction. "Acting would be out of the question," she continued. "Do you think it possible for a lady to, perhaps, write a play?"

"Unexceptionable," he admitted. "Even the Religious Tract Society couldn't object. Your mentor, Hanna More, turned her fine hand to it, with considerable success, I might add."

"I wonder if I could do it." Pamela mused.

Breslau was a trifle put out that the young lady was at so little pains to institute a flirtation. In this mood he said, "You're too young, and unaware of life to try it for a few years yet. One must live before she puts her experiences to paper."

"Nigel has no more experience than I have," she snipped, and turned her head away to show Breslau she was unhappy with him.

He was quite simply amazed to find himself ignored by a country miss whom he had honored with his attentions. Not only ignored, she went out of her way to argue with him! She actually found it conceivable that standing up with him was an unpleasant duty. His eyes slid down to her profile, and he found himself gazing at a small, shell-like ear, as dainty as a newborn babe's. A thick chestnut curl nestled on the ivory nape of her neck. He felt an urge to touch it.

While he sat, entranced at the feelings this farouche young lady was engendering in him, she suddenly turned to face him, and he was struck once more by the beauty of her eyes. "Who's the gentleman with the marquise?" she asked.

He leaned forward and peered through the broad archway, to where Fleur stood in earnest conversation with a young stranger.

"He can't be from Hatfield. I've never seen him," Pamela said. She had the countryman's eager interest in strangers. Added to it was the bonus that this particular stranger was young and handsome, and wearing a jacket of a cut seldom seen in the country.

Breslau felt a burning sensation in his chest. Jealousy was a stranger to him; he thought it was merely annoyance at the interruption in their conversation. "Would you like to be presented to him?" he asked, intending sarcasm.

She immediately bounced to her feet. "I should like it of all things. Do hurry, Lord Breslau, he's leaving."

By the time they reached the ballroom, the man had left, and a group of locals were shyly shimmying forward to compliment the Flawless Fleur.

"Too late," Pamela said, and looked around for some other group to join.

Breslau placed a firm but gentle hand on her elbow to lead her back to the refreshment parlor.

"Let's stay here," she suggested. "There's no one in the refreshment parlor. We'd be all alone, and I haven't found a partner for the next set yet."

Breslau smiled in rising dudgeon and remained in the ballroom. So the lump spurned the opportunity of being alone with him! Had God sent her to teach him a lesson? Miss Comstock had soon attracted another gentleman's eye. A callow youth approached, and she smiled in apparent pleasure at someone called Ethan, wearing a jacket Breslau wouldn't have tolerated on his servants.

"I hear the marquise is putting up with the Raleighs," the young man said. "What's she like, Pam?"

"Not nearly as dashing as I had hoped," Pamela replied, and began to regale him with some anecdotes.

Breslau coldly excused himself and left, perfectly aware that he wouldn't be missed one iota. He made a firm resolution not to honor Miss Comstock with another dance, and stuck with it till after dinner, which was a perfectly hideous affair. Fleur was in one of her moods, and became louder and less polite as the meal advanced. She flirted with every yahoo who stopped at the table to meet her.

The more she flirted the stiffer Lady Raleigh's face grew, till in the end she couldn't get her mouth pried open to eat anything. A delicious cream bun grew soft on her plate, and cream buns were one of her few weaknesses. The Maxwell table was about the only one in the room that wasn't staring at Lady Chamaude with varying degrees of ire or admiration or mirth. No eye at the general's table was allowed to come within a right angle of the actress.

"An intolerable evening," was Lady Raleigh's opinion when they reached home, and for a change, her husband agreed with her.

"I have a splitting headache," she said. "The youngsters will remain belowstairs for a half hour or so. Breslau will play propriety. If I am with that creature for another moment, I shall crown her."

She informed Breslau of his duty and retired abovestairs at once. He was incensed to hear himself relegated to the role of chaperone, but concealed it like the well-bred gentleman he was. Sir Aubrey accompanied his dame upstairs. He thought the open doorway was an oversight. Dot had specifically mentioned she had a headache. He wouldn't inopportune her at this critical juncture. He'd need all her goodwill to explain a few matters.

The marquise had only a glass of wine before retiring. "I'll look over chapter four before sleeping," she said to Nigel. "Tomorrow morning we'll get busy on it. I expect you'll find more broken sentences. He is always teasing me about my poor grammar," she explained. "Say ten o'clock in the library?"

Nigel smiled a blissful smile. "I'll be waiting." He sighed, then turned to the guests. "Well, this visit ain't going as badly as you thought it would, Wes."

"No, it is going worse," Breslau replied, and helped himself to wine. He brought a glass to Pamela, which she set aside, untouched, though she did give him the echo of a smile for his thoughtfulness. It was enough encouragement that he sat beside her.

Any notion of proceeding with the flirtation was soon dispatched. His charges had other matters on what they chose to call their minds. Nigel firmly refused to discuss Fleur with Pamela. He held the floor, "trying an idea for the play" out on them.

"I envisage a hero with a surfeit of hubris, and a heroine chockful of altruism to knock the stuffing out of him—philosophically speaking I mean."

"Could you translate that into English?" Pamela asked.

"In simple words that even you could understand, what I have in mind is a confrontation between a man of specious good and a woman of intrinsic merit, who is spurned by society for some reason or other."

"Another simpering, put-upon heroine and a villain for her to tame into a hero," Breslau said wearily. "At least we aren't to be treated to autobiography, the other failing of amateurs. Try for a little originality, Nigel, and a little heart. Fleur aims her arrows south of the neck."

"Eh? You make it dammed hard." He scowled. "The heroine has to be good."

"Good, but not necessarily perfect. And remember, if you're writing for Fleur, make it a comedy."

"Damme, she's told me to make it a tragedy. That's what she wants to do next."

"What she wants is fifty guineas a performance. I told her I know half a dozen fine actresses who'd be happy to work for half that."

"And she knows the half dozen you have in mind—Rose Flanders, that's who. Rose ain't one, two, three with Fleur."

"Couldn't you work out some compromise?" Pamela suggested. "I mean a serious play with some co-medic scenes."

"Oil and water don't mix. Every playwright worth his salt knows that," Nigel told her.

"Does Shakespeare know it?" she demanded hotly.

"*Hamlet* don't exactly have them rolling in the aisles," Nigel riposted.

"What about the grave-diggers' scene? Just write about life, Nigel," she urged. "Everybody's life has some good times and some bad. Fleur's own life certainly has."

"When I want help from an amateur, I'll let you know, Pam," Nigel said haughtily, and walked to the grate to stand with his hand artistically braced on his brow to aid inspiration. He found that the other hand on his waist, pushing back his jacket, added a certain something to the pose.

Pamela gave him a derisive look. Breslau had begun to wonder if it was Miss Comstock's involvement with Nigel that held her back from responding to his advances. She appeared quite concerned at his offering for Fleur. He gave her a laughing look. "You'll not bring him up to scratch by nagging, Miss Comstock."

"I should hope not indeed!"

It seemed she had no interest whatsoever in Nigel, so that couldn't account for her behavior. His eyes rested on her newly arranged hair, and the rather plain gown. Her shawl had been cast aside, revealing an enchantingly lithe figure. "I was beginning to wonder if you hadn't changed your mind when you dared to appear in front of Nigel in such a dashing new style. This isn't the spinster who was scowling at us when we arrived."

"There's no reason I must look a quiz in front of all the other gentlemen just because I don't want Nigel to think I'm pretty," she answered. Her tone was far from flirtatious. It had an angry buzz to it.

"You're regretting the young blade with Fleur, the one who got away?"

Pamela called to enquire of Nigel who the gentleman was. He lifted his head from his hand a moment to reply, "I didn't see any strange men there."

Even when she described him in vigorous detail, Nigel didn't recall seeing him. "Fleur is the only one he spoke to, then he left," she said. "I think he came just to see her. What do you think, Nigel?"

"I think I'll open with a duel."

Pamela scowled at Breslau. "You've created a monster," she charged. "Bad as Nigel was before, I can see his head is going to be swollen to a pumpkin before this play is finished."

"Perhaps it will resume normal proportions when it is rejected."

An angry flare shot from her catlike eyes. "You mean you don't intend to produce it! Breslau, that's horrid! Why on earth did you ask him to write it then?"

"It will be a learning experience for him."

She wished to say a good deal more on the subject, but Nigel was stirring to life at the grate. His hand left his brow and began to draw random figures in the air. His head nodded as though he were speaking to some invisible listener. His lips even moved, though no sounds issued forth.

"Is he having a fit?" Pamela asked.

"A fit of inspiration, I fear."

Nigel turned a beaming face on them. "By Jove,

I've got it, Wes. Listen to this! You'll love it, and so will Fleur. I shall write a dramatization of her memoirs. The woman's had an incredible life. Did you know the Frenchies were after her to spy for them? They hounded her mercilessly. I've been running a few ideas through my mind and come up with the perfect opening. Her arrival at Brighton in the lugger—the crux of the whole thing."

Breslau blinked. "How did you plan to get an ocean and a lugger onstage?" he asked.

"That's your department. Damme, they had an elephant and sixteen horses in *Bluebeard,* and made money on it, too. It was a roaring success."

"But still, an ocean . . ."

"A painted ocean," Pamela suggested.

"She's got the idea," Nigel agreed, with the first smile shown Pamela since her arrival.

"It's an interesting notion," Breslau admitted. "The publicity from the book and play would feed each other, and to have Fleur playing herself—yes, it has comedic possibilities."

"By the living jingo, it's perfect!" Nigel said. "Fraught with—with everything. I'll even put in a little comedy to please you, Wes. The scene where Fleur is escaping in the cart of turnip—now that could be humorous, in a bloodcurdling sort of way."

"You said it was going to open with her arrival at Brighton," Pam reminded him.

"We're in the preliminary stages. "I'm not sure Paris ain't the place to start. The crux of the whole thing. She had some pretty good stuff in her opening chapter."

"You could paint the backdrop of Paris, too," Pam said hastily.

65

Breslau found another objection. "Before you go any further, Nigel, you really ought to discuss it with Fleur. If the plan is to dramatize her book, then she'll have to approve it. She'll expect a share of the royalties."

"Dash it, I'll be doing the writing! I've practically rewritten the whole mess, if you want the truth. Honestly, you wouldn't believe what she calls a sentence."

Breslau had heard quite enough of the play, and said rather imperatively, "Still, you'll have to clear it up with her before you go any further. I don't plan to referee a plagiarism suit. You can discuss it tomorrow."

"I'll discuss it now," Nigel announced. "Fleur ain't sleeping."

He flung out of the room and pelted off to her suite.

"Now see what you've done," Pamela scolded. "Lady Raleigh would throw a fit if she knew he was going to her room."

"Who suggested writing from life?" he asked. "Actually it's a good idea. I wonder who I could get to write the play."

"Breslau! Nigel is writing it! You can't pull it out from under him!"

Breslau gave a guilty start, and silently cursed himself. "I meant who could help Nigel put a final polish on it. He's a rank amateur. This idea is too good to risk dwindling to a mediocre melodrama."

Her color rose, and her eyes flashed. "You're a perfect beast!"

"Surely not perfect!" Despite his facetious reply, he knew she was right. He also knew no other lady would have told him so to his face in such angry

66

accents. Before he had time to conciliate her, Nigel was back.

He stood in the doorway, his face the color of snow, and his eyes staring wildly.

"Won't she let you do it?" Pamela asked.

"She's dead," he said in a quaking voice. "She didn't answer when I knocked, so I went in—I wasn't sure she could hear me from the drawing room, so I opened the door, and she was lying on the bed . . . stone . . . cold—dead."

His words petered out to a whisper and his knees buckled. As Pamela and Breslau watched in horror, Nigel sank gracefully to the floor in a faint.

## Chapter Five

"Brandy, Wes. Get him some brandy, and a feather to burn." Pamela jumped up, her arms flailing the air futilely.

Breslau was already rushing toward Nigel. He lifted his head and tapped his pale cheeks lightly. "Bring some wine," he called over his shoulder.

She found it easier to follow one explicit order than to think rationally. She took up her own wineglass and flew to hold it to Nigel's lips. His watery eyes opened and looked up in vague confusion.

"She's dead," he muttered, and gulped the wine.

"She can't be dead," Pamela said. "She was hale and hearty not fifteen minutes ago."

"Damme, I know death when I see it," Nigel scowled, and with assistance from Breslau, he gained his feet.

"Could she be foxed?" she asked.

Breslau shook his head. "Fleur's not much of a drinker. She quacks herself with laudanum when she can't sleep. That could be it.

"She wasn't trying to sleep. She was working on

chapter four," Nigel reminded them. "If you don't believe she's dead, go and see for yourself."

"I have no intention of charging into the lady's chamber on such a fool's errand," Breslau stated. "You might have a look, Pamela, if you're worried." In the excitement of the moment, first names cropped out unthinkingly, without their even noticing it.

"I think I should," she said, and went down the hall. Her insides were shaking, but the marquise was so very lively it was impossible to think of her being dead. In his confusion, Nigel had left the door ajar. Pamela tapped, and when there was no answer, she pushed the door inward.

By the dim light of the dresser lamp she could see there was no body on the bed, and a tide of relief washed over her.

"Lady Chamaude," she called toward the connecting room. "Are you all right?" There was no answer. Pamela advanced to the drawing room, where a lamp flickered in a gush of cold air. The door to the outdoors was open six inches, blowing lightly in the wind. The drawing room was empty. The folder of hand-written memoirs sat unopened on a desk, the pen sat in its holder.

Perhaps she'd felt faint and went out for a breath of air? Pamela hurried to the open doorway and looked all around, calling into the darkness. A fine curtain of rain fell, turning to soft ice as it landed. The sky was a moonless ceiling of silver. Obviously Fleur hadn't gone out on such a night.

Her suite was situated at the back of the house. The door opened on the west side to a stoned and hedged garden. Stripped of its summer flowers, it resembled a small, dark cell, furnished with a stone bench and three large tubs holding black bushes.

As she turned to close the door, Pamela noticed a blot of white in one of the bushes. It looked like snow, but there had been no snow. She made a quick dart into the freezing rain, grabbed up the white thing and returned to the room to examine it. It was a lace-edged handkerchief. No obliging monogram decorated the corner, but a light, musky scent still hung about it.

She closed the door and turned to go back to the saloon. Impatient at the delay, the others had come to join her. She heard Breslau's confident voice in the next room. "Probably sound asleep at her desk," he said.

"You'd best come in here," she called. Walking to the next room seemed beyond her powers.

The faces that soon appeared at the door were alive with curiosity. Nigel's was still bone-white.

"She's not here," Pamela said, and explained her findings. "She must have left, but it's pouring rain. I hope she wore her pelisse at least."

Breslau strode to the study door and disappeared beyond it, into the night.

"Do you recognize this handkerchief?" Pamela asked, and handed the wet cloth to Nigel.

He fingered it forlornly and nodded. "A French needlewoman makes them for her. She always carries one."

"At least she's not dead, Nigel," Pamela comforted him. "I expect she felt weak and went out for air. She must have tripped. You'd best go and help Breslau bring her back."

Nigel went out, and Pamela looked around the

70

room for evidence of Fleur's recent activities. Nothing in the austere room had been disarranged. The window hangings were deep blue, the carpet a tired, old blue-flowered affair. A desk and chair, an uncompromising wooden bench that did not encourage lounging, a table holding dried flowers, and an assortment of undistinguished bibelots were the furnishings. She wandered to the desk and noticed that the pen was dry. Of course, if Fleur had felt weak, she couldn't work. She'd decided to lie down a moment first, and had fainted or fallen asleep.

Pamela went into the bedchamber and took a peep about her. This room was more comfortable than the drawing room. The hangings had been replaced within the last decade in a pretty royal blue. The carved and canopied bed was ornate without being elegant. Its covering was undisturbed except for the dent where Fleur had lain down, and her night things laid out at the bottom of the bed. On the mahogany toilette table, a battery of silver and crystal toilet articles were ranged. Pam went to examine them. Brush, comb, hand mirror, nail clippers, nail file, a suede nail polisher, a miniature sewing set, powder, rouge, perfume. She unscrewed the cap and sniffed—yes, it smelled like the wet handkerchief. What was keeping Nigel and Breslau?

Next she cast a covetous eye on the nightgown and peignoir laid out on the bed. All shiny pink satin and blond lace. The familiar musky scent rose from them. Fleur would wish she'd brought a flanelette nightie with her. The room was freezing, though a sluggish fire smoldered in the grate. On the floor, a pair of high-heeled satin slippers awaited Fleur's dainty toes.

So this was how an actress lived. Pam thought of the comfortable mules and flanelette nightie in her own room. On her dresser rested no battery of crystal and silver but a plain horn-backed brush and comb. No wonder Fleur looked so beautiful. Any woman would if she used all that stuff. What could be keeping them?

Finally becoming bored, she went to the clothespress and peeked in. The only clothing was the green suit Fleur had arrived in. The feathered bonnet rested on the top shelf. She thought Fleur was the sort of woman who would have half a dozen changes of clothes in two days and nights. The sable cape was gone. Fleur must have thrown it over her shoulders before going out for air. Naturally she wouldn't go out in her evening gown.

At last the sound of footfalls and subdued voices was heard in the next room. Pam waited for the men to join her, fully expecting to see Fleur with them. She carefully closed the clothespress door and stood innocently in the middle of the room. When the men came in, she looked from one to the other, bewildered.

"Where is she?" she demanded.

"We couldn't find her," Nigel said.

"You have to find her, Nigel. She's fainted, out in that cold rain. She'll catch pneumonia."

At this point, Pamela noticed that Breslau looked—not quite guilty, but somehow *knowing.* "What's going on? What haven't you told me?" she demanded.

"It will be best if we continue our discussion in the saloon," he answered, and took Pamela's elbow to lead her to the door.

She shook him off impatiently. "If she's missing,

we should notify someone. Did you find any trace of her? I don't understand."

"Pam's right," Nigel said. "There's no saying Fleur—"

Breslau gave him a warning glance.

"If you don't tell me this instant, I shall notify your father, Nigel," Pamela stated firmly. It was the likeliest threat to bring him to heel.

"We might as well tell her," Nigel said. "She's like a dog with a bone, Wes. We'll not get a moment's peace till she knows everything. We certainly don't want Papa making a fuss. And Mama! Lord, she'd have me filleted and fed to the vultures. I hope Fleur has the sense to get back before dawn."

"Where has she gone?" Pamela demanded, her voice rising.

"You tell her, Wes. I have to run up to my room for a moment."

Nigel vanished, and Pamela allowed herself to be returned to the saloon on the understanding that she would be told all. Breslau, that mountain of confidence, appeared decidedly ill at ease.

"There's nothing for you to worry about. Fleur has gone to visit a—a friend," he said.

She pinned him with a disbelieving stare. "The vicar?" she enquired in a tone of heavy irony.

"Hardly."

"I didn't come down in the last rain, Breslau. Ladies don't go slipping out in the dead of night in the freezing rain to pay a social call. Now what is really going on?"

Breslau was unaccustomed to such brash behavior from young ladies, and pokered up. "If you insist on knowing, she's gone to visit a gentleman," he said curtly.

Pamela's eyes opened wide. For a moment she was speechless, then she asked, in a squeaky voice, "A love tryst, do you mean?"

"That's a somewhat Elizabethan turn of phrase, but you've got the general idea."

"Who?"

"She didn't leave a note."

"Then you don't know for sure. How could she be having a rendezvous? She doesn't know anyone here."

"Fleur has a broad circle of acquaintances throughout the country."

"A woman wouldn't go to such uncomfortable rounds for a mere acquaintance. I wonder if it's that handsome young stranger she was talking to at the assembly."

"Very likely."

"But he doesn't live around here or Nigel would have recognized him. She wouldn't meet him at the public inn, surely. She's not that rackety, is she, Breslau?"

"We had achieved a first-name basis a while back," he pointed out with an arch look designed to divert her thoughts.

It failed miserably. Pamela was scrambling through her mind and hit unerringly on the culprit. "General Max!" she exclaimed. "I knew there was something havey-cavey going on."

"The slander is in your dish, madam. I didn't mention names. And it would be better if you not air your suspicions to your hostess."

She glared. "I'm not a complete Johnnie Trot."

"If you'd care to have a seat, Miss Comstock, then you would permit me to do likewise. I'm tired, at the end of a long day."

"Oh, for heaven's sake, sit down. I think better when I pace."

She began pacing up and down in front of the grate, while Breslau followed her silently with his eyes. The light from the grate struck her curls, burnishing them with copper highlights. Divested of her shawl, Pamela's slender figure made a pretty sight as she paced back and forth, like a preacher preparing his sermon. After a few turns, she drew to a stop in front of Breslau's chair.

"That can't be right," she said. "General Max wouldn't dare invite her to his house, nor take her to a local inn. His mother is as bad as Lady Raleigh. As good, I mean," she said hastily when Breslau's thin lips lifted in a smile.

"Then we must assume he had his carriage waiting nearby and carried her a little further afield."

"I doubt very much if she'd oblige him after the cool way he treated her tonight. She's no doormat, Breslau, and she was furious."

"I'm aware of that. Apparently he sent her a billet-doux sometime during the assembly to patch up the rift and arrange the, er—love tryst."

Pamela considered this for feasibility, and was still unconvinced. "It is all exceedingly odd. Can they possibly be that eager to—to see each other," she said primly, "that they couldn't wait till she returns to London?"

A sardonic gleam lit his pale eyes. "You will find, as you succumb to some suitor's charms, Miss Comstock, that 'seeing each other' can be inconveniently urgent."

"Inconvenience must have reached its apogee tonight. Mrs Maxwell was fully alert and on the warpath. She keeps the general on a two-inch leash when he's home, you must know."

"Which no doubt accounts for his spending so much time in London."

"The inconvenience wasn't all on his side. It was no easy matter for Fleur to get to him in this pelting rain." She paused a moment, then emitted a squeak. "Breslau, that's why she wanted the downstairs suite!" she exclaimed.

It was Fleur's insistence on wanting that particular set of rooms that pretty well convinced Pamela. Nigel returned, frowning into his collar.

"You didn't tell your father?" Pamela asked.

"Of course not! Do you take me for an idiot? Anyway, he's sound asleep." He turned to Breslau, who was regarding him oddly. "Did you tell her?"

"She knows," Breslau answered noncommittally.

Lord Breslau pulled out his watch and glanced at it. "It's one o'clock," he said. "Time we all retire."

Pamela chose that moment to take a seat. She sat with her chin resting on her hands. The puckering of her brow indicated deep thought. "It's odd Fleur didn't extinguish the lamps before she left."

"We've already discussed the urgency of the tryst," Breslau reminded her.

She gave him an angry look. "And she left the door open, too."

"She has to get back in before dawn, numbskull,"

76

Nigel retorted. "Did you leave the door on the latch, Breslau?"

"Certainly I did."

"But she didn't just leave it on the latch. She left it hanging open," Pamela told them. "A great gust of wind hit me when I went into the drawing room. Now that is odd, don't you think?"

"You're trying to make bricks without straw here, Miss Comstock," Breslau said dismissingly.

A frown pinched Nigel's brow. "She *did* look very dead, Wes," he said uncertainly. "She was cold as ice."

"Two lumps of coal don't give off much heat. The room was like an icehouse."

"Yes, but she was colder than that," Nigel insisted. "If she wasn't dead, she was unconscious. She didn't bat an eyelash when I jiggled her arm and tried to waken her. How did she wake up and sneak out so quickly?"

"You forget, Nigel, the lady's an actress. She didn't want to waste time talking to you, and pretended she was sleeping to be rid of you."

"Why didn't she lock her door to keep anyone from the house going in?" Pamela asked.

Nigel was only half-listening. He appeared very worried, but after a moment he said, "There isn't any lock on that door."

"Was she wearing her sable cape when you saw her, Nigel?" Pamela asked.

"No, she was just lying on top of the counterpane. Why do you ask?"

"Because I checked her room, and her cape's missing. Since the room's so cold, you'd think she would have thrown it over herself. And another thing, her night things are still on the bed."

Pamela had very little idea what degree of formality existed during a love tryst, but thought the peignoir at least might have been required. "That's rather odd, isn't it?" she asked, directing her question to Nigel.

"Don't look at me! Ask Wes."

"They aren't required, though ..." Breslau stopped in midspeech and turned to Pamela. "What else was left behind?"

"All her toilet articles—brush, comb, powder, rouge—they were on the toilette table. She'd need them. Her hair would be all mussed after—after she got up," she finished, with a rebukeful glance at Breslau, who was watching her with a smile.

"Was her reticule gone?" he asked.

"I didn't notice."

Without further conversation they all returned to Fleur's suite. They lit the lamps and made a cursory search of the room. Fleur's beaded evening bag was found on a chair, and the larger leather reticule she'd brought with her was on the shelf of the clothespress, along with her bonnet.

"That's the bonnet she wore this afternoon," Nigel exclaimed. "She didn't bring any other hatbox with her. Dash it, Wes, she wouldn't have gone jauntering off without her bonnet or reticule."

"This suggests an *incredible* urgency," Pamela agreed, and looked to Breslau for explanation.

He lifted the reticule and drew out the wallet. "Her money's here."

"See if General Max's billet-doux is there," Pamela suggested.

"What billet-doux?" Nigel demanded. "Did that old goat write to her?"

"We shouldn't be rooting through her things," Breslau said.

"Damme, she could be murdered for all we know," Nigel exclaimed. "Take a look, Wes. I want to see that letter."

Breslau dumped the contents of the reticule and beaded evening bag on the counterpane. The usual feminine miscellany was there, but no letter from General Max, and nothing to give a reason for Fleur's abrupt departure.

Pamela glanced at the contents, then looked around the room. "I notice her favorite shawl is missing."

Nigel stood, biting his underlip as though he wanted to say something. At last he could control himself no longer and blurted out, "That ain't all that's missing."

"What do you mean?" Pamela asked.

"Nothing. Fleur's missing, too. And I don't believe for one minute she went to see Maxwell. She didn't walk out of here on her own feet, not when she was lying stiff as a board and stone-cold two minutes before. Somebody killed her, and took the body away to hide."

"That strikes me as extremely unlikely," Breslau said. "Before we sound any alarm, we must review the matter. Fleur's chamber wasn't that far from the saloon. We didn't hear any disturbance. There'd have been a racket if someone tried to jump her. She would have screamed when she was attacked. You didn't see any blood?"

"Lord, no," Nigel said. "She looked very peaceful."

"There's no sign of an intruder—nothing in the room is disarranged," Breslau pointed out, looking around. "It was an orderly departure. Fleur won't thank us for calling the police in."

"I don't like it," Nigel insisted.

"No more do I," Breslau agreed. "But we shall wait till morning and see if she isn't back in her room."

"He's right, Nigel," Pamela said. "I believe Fleur's lover—General Max, or the handsome stranger who was not necessarily a stranger to *her*—came tapping at her door. She didn't want anyone to hear, so she picked up her pelisse and went out to speak to him. He convinced her to go off somewhere, and she went. She'll probably be back any moment."

"You don't fool me, Pam. You're just trying to show me Fleur ain't the sort of lady I should marry," Nigel charged.

"Surely you can see that for yourself."

"Pamela's right," Breslau said firmly. "The thing to do is for us to go to bed, before your mother comes down to see what's keeping us. If Fleur isn't back by morning, then we'll begin making serious enquiries."

"I, for one, am going to bed," Pamela said, and made her good nights before leaving.

Breslau went into the hall and watched her mount the stairs. When she was gone, he returned to Nigel. "I'd like to hear a little more about what else is missing," he said, "and why you felt it necessary to dash up and make sure your father was in his room. Was he, by the by?"

"Of course he was! I couldn't say anything in front of Pam. The worst thing, Wes. Fleur stole Mama's diamond bracelet.

Breslau looked blank. "Good God, man, she's not a thief! Where did you get that idea?"

"She had it on her wrist. I'd recognize it anywhere. It's an antiquated old thing, with a diamond link chain and an ugly old flower in the middle. Quite distinctive. All Fleur's jewelry is of the latest cut."

"How could she steal it? Your mother didn't wear it this evening. Where is it kept?"

"In the safe in Papa's office. That's why I went to see Papa, to ask if he'd given it to her, but he was asleep. I can't imagine how Fleur got in and opened the safe. And why she only stole the bracelet and left the necklace," he added, sinking deeper into confusion. "At least she wasn't wearing Mama's necklace."

Breslau pinched his aching temples and sighed. "Oh, Lord. It was bad enough that Fleur was carrying on with Max at such a time and place. Now it seems the wretched woman has turned her hand to blackmail."

"Papa didn't even know I wanted to marry her. And Mama couldn't have given her the bracelet, for she don't know how to open the safe."

"Nigel, you clothhead. You're making an ass of yourself, dangling after Fleur." But, of course, this was not the matter Fleur was using for her illicit ends.

"You're just jealous."

"Go to bed. We'll talk in the morning. And I'll see that Fleur returns the bracelet."

"Who could sleep with all this weighing on him," Nigel said, and went to fetch the wine bottle, for it was clear he and Wes had some heavy man-to-man talk coming up.

# Chapter Six

It took considerable ingenuity on Breslau's part to convince Nigel he had imagined seeing the bracelet and dissuade him from discussing it with his father. The delusion was blamed on the excitement of literary creation.

"Any dramatist worth his salt sees imaginary scenes of incredible clarity when he is creating," Breslau explained.

"That's true." Incredibly lifelike scenes between himself and Fleur had been popping quite unbidden into his mind.

"You were in the throes of literary inspiration. Very fatiguing work, I should think. Let us retire now, so you'll be fresh in the morning."

Eventually Nigel was persuaded up to bed, but it was more than an hour before his cot in the next room fell silent and Breslau was free to return belowstairs. His mood boded ill for the wayward marquise. It stung his pride to skulk about like a character in a French farce, creeping downstairs in his stocking feet, peering all about to make sure no one was watching him. If Lady Raleigh should take into her head to patrol the hallway, for instance, she'd jump to the wrong conclusion. Or Miss Comstock, for that matter.

He reached the downstairs landing without incident and proceeded silently along the hallway toward Fleur's apartment. As he crept along, he heard a squawk from the end of the hall and slid into the closest doorway. From the concealing shadows, he saw a taper moving down the dark hall. In the beam of its flickering light, Sir Aubrey's angry face hovered, looking for all the world like a gargoyle. The squawk, and Sir Aubrey, had both issued from Fleur's apartment door.

Breslau remained hidden till he had passed, then hastened along to the door. The apartment was in total darkness. He called once in a low voice, got no answer, and lit a taper. The rooms were unchanged from his last visit. He was in no mood for sleep, and went to the saloon to await Fleur's return, passing the time with a cheroot, a glass of wine, and his thoughts. When he felt the lassitude of sleep falling on him two hours later, he went upstairs to bed.

Lady Raleigh kept early hours at Belmont. She habitually rose at seven, but allowed her guests to breakfast anytime before nine. At eight, Pamela was at the table alone in a state of high fidgets. When Breslau joined her later, he knew by her staring eyes that more unpleasant surprises were in store.

With a dark look he said, "Don't tell me till I've had a cup of coffee."

"You look awful," Pamela told him. "Did you not sleep?" Breslau's eyes were bleary and smudged with fatigue, but it was the grim set of his lips that gave him that forbidding air.

"Perhaps twenty winks."

As he sipped his coffee, he observed that the night's activities left no trace on Miss Comstock. She looked even brighter and fresher than before, like a healthy animal. After Breslau had drunk half a cup of coffee, she could wait no longer.

"Fleur isn't in her room," she said.

The sounds Breslau uttered were very subdued, and very profane. He had warned Fleur a dozen times that this wasn't the sort of house where she could play off her stunts. Propriety was the watchword here, and she had *promised* to tow the line.

"I hope you haven't told anyone?"

"No, but there's more, Breslau. All her things are gone. I went to her apartment at seven. The room is stripped bare of all her belongings. Lady Raleigh thinks she's still here. I didn't know what to do. I didn't think you'd lie in bed so late on a day like this," she said accusingly.

Breslau stared into the black iridescence in his cup and wished he could be swallowed up in it. Here was a pretty kettle of fish!

"What are you going to do?" she asked.

"Wring her neck when she returns."

"She surely won't have the gall to show her face here again! The removal of her clothing suggests she's returned to London, don't you think? And not even a note of thanks. I call that rag-mannered."

"Is Sir Aubrey up yet?"

"In his study."

Without another word, Breslau went to confront Sir Aubrey. He got his ears singed for his impertinence.

"How dare you suggest I gave that hussy my wife's diamonds!"

"Just the bracelet. At least that's all that was seen." Fortunately Sir Aubrey didn't ask who had seen it. "She had it, Aubrey. You either gave it to her, or she stole it. If it was the latter, I assume you'll be sending for the constable."

"The bracelet is in London being cleaned," Sir Aubrey said stiffly. The livid hue of his jowls might have been due to indignation, or lying.

Breslau wanted to gain his host's trust and assumed a conciliating manner. "I'm not suggesting you're having an *affaire* with the marquise. If you were, it's nothing to do with me. Truth to tell, I feared she was holding you to ransom."

The livid jowls retained their hue, but Sir Aubrey's angry eyes assumed a new wariness. "What are you suggesting she could possibly have against me?"

"Ancient history. From the hints she was tossing your way yesterday, I'd say a liaison in Brighton twenty odd years ago. Am I correct?"

"Certainly not. If I ever knew the woman, I don't recall it. It's true my youth was not as spotless as Lady Raleigh would like, but I was not so abandoned that I forgot my partners."

"Then why did you visit her room late last night?"

"Who says I did!" Sir Aubrey exclaimed, ready to deny it with his dying breath.

"I say so. I saw you leave."

"Hmph. If you must know, I just wished to have a word with her in private."

"I'm afraid you must tell me what that word was."

86

Sir Aubrey froze. "You overstep the bounds of a guest, sir."

"My leading lady is missing. Every journal in London will run banners two-inches high if we don't find her before tomorrow night's performance. She disappeared while under your roof, and in theory, at least, your protection."

"You were her escort!"

"Nigel saw her safely to her apartment."

An impasse had been reached. Sir Aubrey was not ready to confess.

"Can you at least give me your assurance that you didn't ask her to leave your house?"

"Good God, man! I'm not a savage. I was as surprised as you when I saw that empty room."

"You've no idea where she is then?"

"London would be my guess, and good riddance."

London, however, was a two-hour drive away. Breslau knew that if he went to London and didn't find her, he'd have to turn around and come back to Belmont. Better to exhaust all possibilities here first.

"We'll not disturb Lady Raleigh with any unfounded conjectures. I plan to tell her Lady Chamaude was called away suddenly," Sir Aubrey said. His tone was more civil than before.

"What do you plan to tell the constable?"

"No need to call him till you check in London." Sir Aubrey's tone was more than civil, it was pleading, and his eyes wore a haunted look.

"I'm not going to London just yet," Breslau said, and left the study. Let Raleigh stew a while. The sharp edge of fear might loosen his tongue.

Before calling on General Maxwell, Breslau wanted to check Fleur's apartment for himself. He saw Pamela had left the breakfast table, and wasn't surprised to find her already in Fleur's bedroom.

"What did Sir Aubrey say?" she asked.

"Nothing of any account. We plan to tell Lady Raleigh Fleur was urgently summoned to London."

Pamela pointed to the empty clothespress. "Everything's gone, just as I said. Hat, suit, reticule, toilet things. She left the manuscript behind. That's all."

Breslau glanced around the room. "It looks like a hurried job. Drawers left hanging open, clothes hangers on the floor."

"It wouldn't take long. She only brought one evening gown with her, as well as the suit she wore, of course."

"That's odd! Fleur's quite a peacock."

"Well, her maid had a cold and couldn't come with her, so perhaps . . . But it is odd she left no note for her hostess. You know the marquise well, Breslau. Is she likely to have gone off voluntarily without so much as a thank you note?"

Breslau frowned into the distance. "What you're asking is whether I think she left freely, or was kidnapped."

"Actually it was murder I had in mind. Nigel said—"

"You don't have to remind me."

"And we went calmly up to bed without lifting a finger to help her. I feel awful, so guilty. What shall we do, Breslau?"

"I'm going to do a little checking up in the immediate neighborhood before going to London."

"I want to help."

"You and Nigel might drive into the village. Don't

ask pointed questions, but a neighborly chat should tell you whether anyone there saw her leave."

"Nigel! I'm not going with *him*. Where are *you* going?"

"To call on General Maxwell."

"I'll go with you," she said.

"I think not."

"You'll have a better chance for private conversation with General Max if I go along and divert his mother."

"That's true. Very well, I plan to leave immediately."

"I'll tell Lady Raleigh. Nigel's still sleeping, so she won't object."

Within minutes they were ensconced in Breslau's comfortable chaise. The temperature had risen enough that last night's ice had melted. Beyond the window, dreary winter's landscape was at its unloveliest, but neither of them glanced out the window. They were too engrossed in the mystery.

"If General Max has left, will you assume he's carried Fleur off to London?" she asked.

"It would suggest it. I'll have to follow them."

Pamela saw the excitement evaporating before her very eyes. With Breslau and the marquise gone, it would be just another boring visit. "I am to go to London tomorrow, to pay a short visit to my Aunt Foster before returning to Kent," she said musingly. "If I went with you today, it would save Sir Aubrey having his team put to. Nigel was supposed to accompany me. We could both go with you."

"I shan't be going unless General Max has gone. You're welcome to accompany me whenever I go, however. Even if Fleur's with me, there'll be room for another in the carriage. In fact, I don't see why any other arrangement was ever considered."

"Lady Raleigh wouldn't permit me to travel with Fleur. I wonder if—no, she can hardly object to my traveling with you," she decided.

Breslau said not a word, but his eyes spoke volumes. Now it was a slur on his character! "You do me too much honor, Miss Comstock."

"I shall have Nigel to protect me." The laughter lurking in her eyes was all that saved her from a setdown.

"There is the flaw in the plan, eh, Miss Comstock?"

"It's hardly a flaw. He won't call on me once I'm at Foster's, but I do hope *you* will, Lord Breslau." A flash of surprise lit his pale eyes. Was it possible the girl had at last tumbled to it that he was an extremely eligible *parti*? "Otherwise I'll never hear what happened to Fleur," she added, unconscious of causing offense.

So much for romance! "My hope is that we'll know that as soon as we call on Maxwell."

Before the visit had properly begun, Breslau had a pretty good notion it was a fruitless one. General Maxwell was at home, reading to his mother, and was very much surprised to receive the visitors.

"You've brought Miss Comstock to call on Mama," he said, putting his own interpretation on the visit.

"Delighted to see you, Pamela," the dame said, and patted the sofa beside her. "Come and tell me all about your visit to Belmont."

Before long, General Max had invited Breslau into the Armaments Room, ostensibly to admire his gun collection. The conversation soon turned to more interesting matters.

"I daresay Fleur is unhappy with me," Max said sheepishly. All his military bluster was gone, leaving him a trembling shadow of himself. "I asked her not to come here. She knows how unreasonable my mother is."

"I'm afraid she is unhappy, Max. She left last night."

"Good," he said, and drew forth a handkerchief to wipe his brow. "When you return to London, tell her I'll call on her the minute I arrive. I won't be going till next week. Mama has some estate business that I must take care of."

"You didn't pass Fleur a billet-doux last night then?"

"I hadn't a moment's privacy after my sister sounded the alarm. Bossy old shrew. The ladies are all alike. They take Fleur in aversion without knowing a thing about her. I would marry Fleur if I could, Breslau. I've told her so times out of mind. If only she will be patient. While Mama is alive, you know . . ."

"I'm familiar with the problem."

"It's not that I don't love her—and respect her! I'll give her a little gift, that should do the trick."

Breslau was convinced the general knew nothing, and saw no point in alarming him. They rejoined the ladies, and as soon as decently possible, the guests left.

"Max had no idea she's missing," he said when they were once more in the carriage.

"Then there's only one more thing to do before we

set out for London. We must make those enquiries in the village."

"Enquiries will only start gossip. We chat, and keep our ears cocked for anything of interest. Someone might mention seeing her leave."

"We should also make enquiries about the handsome stranger Fleur was talking to. You know, the one—"

"The one I failed to present you to. Keep an eye out for him as well."

"The first stop will be the drapery shop," Pamela said. "All the gossips will be meeting there to discuss the ball. I know several of them."

Breslau was not thrilled to spend his morning in a drapery shop, but Pamela's plan was a good one. Before long he found himself looking over the ells of silk and wool.

"How dear woolens are becoming," she scolded. "Ah, Mrs. Williams! I see you have recovered from the assembly. Lovely, was it not?"

"The whole village is agog with the lovely marquise." Mrs. Williams smiled. "She isn't with you?" she asked, peering hopefully over Pamela's shoulder.

"No."

"The likes of her would have her clothes from London or Paris. She turned out very elegant last night, but not gaudy."

After four meetings and four queries from the locals for the marquise, Breslau took Pamela's elbow. "We're wasting time. No one saw her leave, or the village would know it."

"You're right. It's time to begin looking for the handsome stranger. I've made a few discreet enquiries. No one knows him. He was only in and out of the assembly for ten minutes. It looks as though he went there especially to see Fleur."

This shadowy gentleman figured very little in Breslau's suspicions, but as all other leads had run dry, he was willing to consider him. "We'll make enquiries at the two inns," he said.

"Why should we tip our hand?" she asked sagely. "First let us go on the strut. If we spot him on the street, we can follow him to his lair."

"You envisage a morning of high melodrama, I see. Very well, once up and down the street, then we hit the inns."

Pamela took his arm. "We don't want to look suspicious," she explained. "Pretend we're just out for a stroll. How the old cats will gossip." She smiled. "They'll think you've beat Nigel out and won my hand."

Her careless laugh made a joke of it. Again Breslau felt that burning in his chest. Why was it that Miss Comstock remained totally oblivious to his eligibility? His first suspicion that she was trying to capture his interest by a show of indifference had faded long since. That trick was as familiar as an old ballad; it was accompanied by flirtatious glances and smiles. Miss Comstock employed no such artifices.

"Lady Raleigh will regret inviting me," he said, and looked closely for her reaction. It was an excellent opportunity for her to assure him she had no such regrets.

"Never fear, Breslau, she would contrive to lay the whole in the marquise's dish. Do you see our mystery gentleman?" she asked, looking all around the busy street.

After a turn up one side and down the other, they

were convinced there wasn't a city jacket outside of Breslau's in the whole village.

"Now we'll follow my original idea and check the inn," Breslau said.

"I can describe the man accurately. He had sleek black hair and smoldering eyes, like black coffee. One eyebrow, the left, quirked up a little. His nose was—well, it was very handsome," she sighed.

When they went to the desk of the Rose and Thorn, Breslau asked if a youngster from London had registered yesterday. "Average height, black hair, a dapper-looking fellow."

No such man had set foot in the inn. At the George they fared a little better. He hadn't registered, but a man whom the waitress called "fine as a star, dressed to the nines" had dined there the evening before and asked where the assembly hall might be found. "When I got off work about midnight, I seen him in a fine chaise all alone. I made sure he'd be headed off to Lunnon, but he drove north out of Hatfield."

"Toward Belmont," Pamela said.

"That's right. I expect he's a friend of the Raleighs. That's where you'd find 'un."

"Thank you. You've been very helpful," Breslau said, and handed her a coin.

They hastened out of the inn. "I told you so!" Pamela beamed. "She made a rendezvous with the Adonis. They must have gone to London, don't you think?"

"I don't know where else they could have gone. I'll leave for London immediately."

"Oh, good! It won't take me a minute to pack!"

They returned to Belmont at a smart clip. Pamela's head was full of the projected trip. Now that she'd met the marquise, she meant to badger her Aunt Foster or her brother Harley into taking her to a performance at Drury Lane. Breslau was silently going over the recent events.

He decided Fleur had come to Belmont in an effort to show Max she was respectable enough to marry. His cold reception at the assembly had killed that notion, and in a fit of pique she'd made an assignation with the handsome stranger. But why was the stranger at the assembly? Fleur hadn't asked him to come, not when she hoped to get an offer from Max. And if she had decided to turn respectable, why dun Aubrey for the diamond bracelet? She'd done that before Max offended her.

If the assistance of another man had been foreseen, it would surely be Mr. Spiedel Fleur chose for the job. This handsome young drifter was often seen in her company. Outside of his looks, he had little enough to recommend him. He had no fortune, no known family, and no particular talents. Spiedel had hinted once or twice that he'd like to try his hand at acting. Fleur didn't support this plan at all, and nothing had come of it.

Beslau shook himself to attention, suddenly realizing that Pamela was talking to him. "I expect a director has tickets at his disposal, if the theater is sold out, I mean," she said. The question in her eyes told him he had missed something.

"Yes, er—were you planning to visit the theater, Miss Comstock?"

"Haven't I just said so, twice?"

"I will be very happy to give you tickets. How many do you require?"

"I can hardly go alone. My Aunt and Uncle Foster would be accompanying me."

"My wits are gone begging. You must use my box. I'll bring the tickets around for you. Where do your aunt and uncle live?"

"On Half Moon Street, at the corner of Curzon. Would it be possible for us to go backstage and meet the marquise? Uncle Foster would love it of all things."

"Entirely possible, if Fleur's performing. She had two nights off, you recall. I hope by tomorrow evening . . ."

"You're not still worried about her?"

"A few things puzzle me," he admitted, but didn't go into details.

When the carriage pulled up in front of Belmont, the front door flew open and Nigel came darting out. His pale face was drawn and haggard. "Mama told me you had gone to Maxwell's. Did you find out anything?" he asked.

"The general doesn't know anything," Breslau replied.

"We think Fleur has returned to London," Pamela added.

"Think again. She's been murdered, just as I said all along. I've found her grave."

# Chapter Seven

Two audible gasps echoed in the carriage. Pamela was the first to recover and fly out the door. "Where is it? We must go at once and see it."

"This way," Nigel said, and headed off for the spinney. "I went for a walk to escape Mama's ranting and stumbled across it."

Breslau wasn't a yard behind them. He caught up and said, "Is there actually a body? . . ."

"No, the villain was interrupted at his work, but there's a grave dug, and Fleur's shawl was in it—all trampled in the mud, Wes. Her beautiful green and rose shawl. I felt like bawling when I saw it. I hid it behind a tree. Mama, you know. We had to tell her Fleur had left, when she didn't appear for breakfast by eleven. Mama went darting straight over to discuss the whole thing with Mrs. Maxwell."

"What's your father doing?" Breslau demanded.

Nigel gave a haughty look. "Nothing. Why do you ask it in that way, as though Papa had anything to do with it? You're thinking of my delusion about Mama's diamond bracelet, I suppose."

Pamela whirled around in surprise. "What do you mean?"

"Nothing," Nigel scowled.

"Did Fleur have it? What do you mean?"

"It was a delusion after too much literary inspiration."

Undeceived, Pamela continued hurling questions. "Did your father give it to her, or did she take it?"

"Damme, how should I know? She had it on her wrist when I went to her room, that's all."

"Oh!" Pamela gasped. "Your father caught her stealing it and shot her. He must have mistaken her for an intruder, Nigel. They'll never hang him for it."

"Now see what you've done," Nigel said accusingly to Breslau.

Breslau gave him a scathing look. "You haven't answered my question. Where is your father now?"

"He was in his study going over his account books last I saw. I don't know what that has to do with anything."

Pamela had hard work keeping up with the gentlemen. Between her shorter legs, hampering skirts, and efforts to avoid the worst of the mud, she fell a few yards behind. The spinney where she often rode seemed menacing today.

The sky hung heavy overhead, and the bushes grabbed at her skirts. Droplets of water fell from the shivering branches, landing with a heavy plop on her shoulders. Her shoes were soaked and her skirt tails muddied. A feeling very like doom was in the air. She ran to catch up with the others, who had stopped just twenty yards into the spinney and stood staring at a hole in the ground. Pamela looked at it and shook her head. It was all a hum.

"Nigel, you clunch! That's only a badger sett. It's been there forever."

"I know that. The badgers were killed eons ago. Mama had the hole plugged up and set the mole catcher after them, for they were getting into the beehives. You know how badgers love honey. I found this shovel here. And take a look at this," he said importantly, pointing into the hole.

Pamela went forward and saw that some fresh digging had been done. One rounded end of the sett had been squared off somewhat. "This is where I found the shawl. I'll get it," Nigel said, and disappeared behind a tree, to reappear in a moment with the familiar paisley object.

It looked very forlorn, all wet and bedraggled, and with its beautiful fringe matted into clumps. Pamela glanced to Breslau to hear his opinion. A shiver ran through her when she saw him reach for the shawl and gaze at it. He swallowed convulsively. He believed it then. He thought Fleur was dead—murdered. A silence grew around them, broken only by the dull plopping of water from the branches, and an occasional birdcall.

She felt a stirring of pity, and didn't know whether it was the image of Fleur, dead and wet and muddied like the shawl, or Breslau's tense, grieving face that caused it. She had thought him a mere fashionable fribble, but he had real feelings after all. He must have been very fond of Fleur. Perhaps he even loved her.

She reached for his hand, and he squeezed her fingers. "There's no body, Breslau," she said gently. "We don't know for sure. Perhaps she got away."

He turned his head and gazed at her. He didn't say anything, but just looked, silent. She imagined his eyes were speaking, saying, Thank you. They had a more gentle air than before. He went toward the grave, still holding her hand, and examined the hole from the edge.

"There are dozens of footprints. They look fresh," he said. "Did you go into the hole, Nigel?"

"No, I just pulled the shawl out."

"We'll need someone here to keep people from disturbing these footprints. They might tell us something."

"They're all men's footprints," Pamela pointed out. She was becoming self-conscious at Breslau's continuing to hold her hand, and withdrew. "Fleur's prints aren't here," she said.

"The dead don't walk," Nigel said in doleful accents. "Whoever killed her carried her here."

"He must have been a strong man. Fleur weighed close to ten stone." The image of General Maxwell darted unbidden into her head. Why would he *dig* a grave, and not use it?

Pamela saw a corner of something gray protruding from some leaves that had blown into one corner. "What's this?" she said, and leaned over to pull it out.

It was a gentleman's fine leather glove, not the common York tan usually seen, but a distinctive gray polished leather. It was a little larger than the average man's glove. She couldn't remember what size hands the mysterious stranger had, but Max's were large and capable.

"Do you recognize it?" she asked the men.

Breslau took it and examined it. "No, but it's unusual. We might be able to discover in London who made it." He wrapped it in the shawl. "Where does the spinney lead?"

"Eventually to Norman Quill's farm," Nigel replied. "There's no point thinking he had anything to do with it. He's one of our most respectable tenants, with a wife and seven kids."

"The road to Hatfield passes close by the spinney, though," Pamela pointed out. "Close enough that I've often heard carriages passing when I was riding in the woods. Whoever took Fleur could have had a carriage waiting. No one would have seen it in the middle of the night. The thing to do is call the constable."

"I expect you're right," Nigel agreed. "Not that old Perry Penman will be able to make anything of it. He's only good for locking up drunks and poachers."

"Then why bother telling him?" Breslau asked. "He knows nothing of Fleur's friends and enemies, her habits and haunts. We'll find her ourselves. There's nothing more to be done here."

"Are you going to London now?" she asked.

"Not immediately. I want to look into a few more things here before leaving."

"What are you going to do?" Pamela asked.

"If Fleur was taken away in a carriage, as we think, it must have been waiting at the side of the road for sometime while the owner went to Belmont to get her, and carried her back through the spinney. The unused grave looks as though he was interrupted before he could bury her, and whoever inter-

101

rupted the burial might have seen the carriage. I assume he didn't see anything else, or there'd be another body here."

"Or the constable around asking questions if someone reported peculiar goings on," Nigel added. "The murderer must have been parked an age. He even dug her grave." Nigel stared once more into the badger sett.

"There wouldn't have been much traffic on the road at that hour of the night," Pamela said.

"Someone returning from the assembly might have seen the carriage. Maxwell, for instance, would have passed that stretch of road on his way home. I'll have another word with Max." As he spoke, Breslau drew out the gray glove and fingered it.

"Nigel, you and I can go into Hatfield and see if we can discover what sort of carriage the mysterious stranger drove," Pamela suggested.

"What mysterious stranger?"

She reminded him of all the details of that gentleman as they returned to Belmont. General Maxwell was driving up as they approached the house.

"This saves me a trip," Breslau said. His eyes glinted like an eagle's as he stared at Maxwell. He stepped forward and said, in a quite ordinary voice, "Are you looking for this, General?" and handed him the gray glove.

Maxwell reached for it, his hand sheathed in an identical glove. "Where did you find this? I was sure I lost it in London."

"It seems you were mistaken. What brings you to Belmont, General? I understand Lady Raleigh is with your mother at the moment."

"It's Lady Raleigh's visit that decided me to come.

102

What's this about Fleur having left without telling anyone? You didn't mention that, Breslau. I assumed it was an orderly retreat, not a rout."

Nigel was too impatient to put up with this game of cat and mouse. "She didn't retreat, she was murdered, and I should like to know what your glove was doing in her grave!"

"Her *grave!*" Maxwell's swarthy face turned to ash, and his eyes stared in disbelief. "What is this puppy talking about?" he demanded of Breslau. If the general was bamming, he was doing an excellent job of it.

"We have no hard evidence that Fleur is dead, but we do suspect she might have been kidnapped," Breslau admitted.

"Young Raleigh said her grave! What is that you're holding? Is it Fleur's shawl?"

Pamela found it suspicious Fleur's lover didn't recognize such a familiar object. But then she'd never believed the shawl to be old.

"It's Fleur's," Breslau said. "About her death—the young are inclined to exaggerate," he added, and outlined the situation with what Pamela found a rather optimistic insistence that Fleur was not dead.

The general had to see the grave cum badger sett for himself. When his first shock had subsided, his old military training came to the fore and he examined everything with a practiced eye. Perhaps this was why Breslau talked down the notion of murder, so that General Max wouldn't be too upset to help. He did know his business.

Heedless of his buckskins and top boots, he got down on his hands and knees and stared at the footprints in the grave. "There was only one man here.

103

You notice the boot prints are all the same size. He left and went that way," he said, looking into the spinney. "There's nothing there but Raleigh's sheep field and Quill's farm. He was obviously taking a shortcut to the road. He must have had his carriage waiting."

"That was our opinion," Breslau agreed.

"When did you notice Fleur was missing?"

"Shortly after midnight."

"That long ago!" Max stopped talking and frowned. "My party left the assembly around twelve-thirty. I remember Sis pointing out a carriage stopped by the roadside near the edge of this spinney. I said we should stop to see if the fellow needed help. Mama took a look and said the carriage wasn't from Hatfield, so we didn't bother offering to help."

"What kind of carriage was it?" Breslau asked.

"Just a dark chaise, with four horses. I know there were four, because Mama mentioned that with a team of four they must have enough grooms and riders to tend to the problem themselves. If it had been a gig, we should have stopped."

"A team of four suggests it was a traveling carriage, something that came from a little distance, I mean," Pamela mentioned.

"From London, certainly," Max agreed. "No one from this neighborhood would have any reason to—"

"Someone has!" Nigel reminded him. "We still haven't heard what your glove was doing in the grave."

"I've no idea. I lost it in London, dropped it at the theater or restaurant. Anyone might have picked it up. You don't suppose he's trying to involve *me*! It would be quite a coincidence if whoever happened to pick it up is the culprit, and wore just one glove. I only lost one."

"Are you quite sure the glove is yours?" Breslau asked.

Maxwell took the muddied glove from his pocket and examined it, even sliding it on his hand. "It's mine all right. I have them made to order from a fellow in Bond Street. My hand is broad but not long-fingered. A peasant's hand, Fleur calls it," he added, staring wanly at the glove.

As Pamela stood watching, she saw his expression firm to manly determination. "We'll catch the bleater, whoever he is. I hope you haven't called in the constable, to make a scandal of it? Penman's worse than useless."

"Precisely our opinion," Breslau nodded. He spoke as a friend, but his glinting eyes suggested suspicions of Maxwell were by no means inactive.

Pamela's instinct was to exonerate the general. He was more upset than the rest of them put together, and when he went on to place the blame in his own dish, she could accuse him of nothing worse than being a laggard in love.

"It's all my fault. If I had married her as she wanted, none of this would have happened. She wanted to visit me, you must know. I told her my mother would never permit such a thing. She said, 'Then I shall visit your closest and most respectable neighbor. *Then* your mother will see I'm not a light skirt.' But the visit only made things worse."

Nigel decided to take offense at this. "The visit had nothing to do with you. Fleur came to work on her memoirs with me."

"Those cursed memoirs. I wish she had never decided to write them. It was for the money, of course. She is always short of blunt."

Yet Pamela knew the marquise was paid the inordinate sum of thirty guineas per performance. The emeralds she wore to the party must have been worth thousands of pounds.

"Fleur doesn't live in a very high style," Nigel objected. "Only a little apartment with one maid and a butler. Of course she keeps a carriage, but she always uses job horses."

"Her maid!" Maxwell exclaimed. "Perhaps Maria knows something."

"She didn't bring her maid," Breslau said. "Maria was unwell."

"That's odd," Maxwell said. "She depends totally on Maria. We're wasting time here. We must get busy and find Fleur. And when we do, I shall put a ring on her finger and march her straight off to the minister. I've kowtowed to Mama long enough. Dash it, I'm not a stripling. I have my officer's half-pay, and a competence from Papa."

"How are we going to find her, though?" Pamela asked.

"I shall institute an enquiry, Miss Comstock," Max said with the utmost confidence.

"Here or in London?"

"I shall begin here. No doubt my search will lead me soon to London."

"I'll leave you in charge then, and I'll go on to London immediately," Breslau said. "I'll ask questions of her friends there, and have a look around her apartment for clues."

"Very good. You would know who to talk to better

than I. A pity she has no family. Fleur has often said her family is her fellow thespians—speak to the other actors. I'll look you up and we'll meet for a conference in London, either this evening or tomorrow. Nigel, I want you to take me to Fleur's rooms and show me exactly how everything was found."

"You show him, Pam. I'm off to London with Wes."

Breslau's sharp eyes turned to Pamela. She saw, or imagined, a gleam of interest. "Actually Breslau has agreed to take me to London," she said, making it sound as normal as possible. "I'm stopping off for a visit with the Fosters on the way home."

"I'm not staying here all by myself," Nigel objected.

"What of the play, Nigel?" Breslau asked. "And the memoirs? They are still at Belmont. This is an excellent opportunity for you to finish editing them, so that you'll be free to get on with the play."

Breslau had swallowed the bitter pill. Nigel would be allowed to write the play. It would be an inspired mediocrity that would appeal to the trite and squalid taste of the masses. He would have to settle for another commercial success.

"But I'll be missing out on all the excitement."

"There'll be plenty of excitment here," General Max promised. "A great deal of reconnaissance work to be done. I can use an aide-de-camp. I must learn who was driving that carriage and team that was parked by the side of the road. It may have stopped at the stableyard."

Pamela gave him a description of the mysterious stranger. "I saw the lad ogling Fleur at the assembly," Maxwell said. "He had a sly air about him. I don't know his name, but he's one of the young set of dandies that dangles after the girls at the theater. No particular friend of Fleur, to my knowledge."

They all returned to Belmont. While Nigel showed General Maxwell the scene of the crime, Pamela dashed off a note to her hostess explaining her early departure, and left it with Sir Aubrey, who remained closed up in his study.

"So you're leaving us, eh, Pamela?" he said, trying to force a smile. "I'll tell Dot. Nigel is going along, too, is he?"

"He's remaining a few days to work on the memoirs."

Sir Aubrey had a feeling Dot wouldn't be happy with this arrangement. He was eager to rid his house of company, however, and didn't try to delay Pamela, but only wished her a safe trip. Within half an hour, she was settled in Breslau's comfortable carriage, with a hundred vital matters to discuss.

"Do you think General Maxwell did it?" was her first question. "He's strong enough to have carried Fleur."

"He didn't hesitate to claim the glove. That works in his favor."

"He was truly shocked and sorry. Imagine a grown man, a general, being led by his mother in the choice of a wife. If Fleur turns up alive, some good will have come of this affair."

"That has already occurred to me," Breslau murmured.

"No, I was wrong. General Maxwell would never marry a thief. Don't forget Fleur stole the diamond bracelet."

"She had the bracelet," he conceded. "Whether it was stolen is another matter."

"I know what you're thinking," Pamela ventured rashly. "Lady Raleigh bribed Fleur to release Nigel."

"My understanding is that only Sir Aubrey had access to the safe where the bracelet was kept."

"He had no reason to give it to her. He didn't know Nigel had actually offered for her, you see."

A satirical glint in Breslau's eye gave Pamela the hint she was off course entirely. "The young tend to plant themselves firmly at the center of things. Look a little further afield, Miss Comstock. Nigel's heinous plan to desert you and marry Fleur isn't necessarily the cause of this brouhaha."

"I'm very happy to hear you say so! I couldn't think of any other reason why the Raleighs would have murdered her. But you are intimating that Sir Aubrey gave her the bracelet, I think. Why would he do such an unprecedented thing?"

Breslau didn't reply verbally. His eyes spoke of a reason that was best not discussed with a young lady. "You think there's something between them?" she asked.

"No, *was*, many years ago, in Brighton. You did overhear the words *quarter day* when they were fighting in Sir Aubrey's study, n'est-ce pas? And we all know what happens on quarter day."

"He didn't have any cash on hand, so he gave her the bracelet. Is she really so depraved that she'd turn her hand to blackmail, Breslau?"

"It was a suggestion merely. The deepest recesses of the female heart remain a mystery to me."

"How can you love a woman like that?"

"*Love* her!" Breslau nearly jumped from his seat. "Don't you? Every other man seems to. You stared at her as if you were memorizing her for all eternity. And you looked very sad at the badger sett, when you were holding her shawl."

"I am fond of Fleur, both as a friend and as my leading lady—onstage, I mean," he added.

Miss Comstock ignored this telling addendum. "What intrigues me about the whole affair is how her belongings got packed up and removed during the night. Who took away her clothes, and why? That would have been easy for Sir Aubrey. We should have searched the attics before leaving."

"A corpse doesn't need a change of clothes," Breslau mused. "If a murderer had got clean away with his crime, why return and gather up her belongings? If it was only a common thief, he would have taken her money and jewels when he made his first call. Nigel told me last night that Fleur wore her emeralds when he first went to her room."

"The clues don't point to common theft. It looks very bad for Sir Aubrey, does it not? He might have hidden her body, and removed her belongings to indicate she had left willingly. He's strong enough to have carried her corpse, too. A thief, on the other hand, would have taken the money and jewels and left the body."

"There's no murder case without a corpse. If the intruder killed her by accident, I can see his spiriting away the body, but the *clothes*? No, that doesn't tally with an unknown intruder. And really killing her at Belmont doesn't point to Aubrey. That would be the *last* place he'd murder her, if he planned to kill her, I mean. He would have followed her to London and done it there. Disappearance doesn't necessarily mean murder, of course."

"But if she's not dead—if she left peacefully, I mean—why did she leave her belongings behind in the first place? Why all this game of cat and mouse with Nigel, pretending she was asleep?"

"It's only conjecture, but for what it's worth, we might consider kidnapping. There was a dismal, cold rain last night. If Fleur fell into a puddle, or was so soaked that her kidnapper feared she might take pneumonia . . ."

"Yes," she agreed doubtfully. "He wouldn't want her to die, or he couldn't collect the ransom. But why not just grab a blanket and wrap her in that? Another flaw in the kidnapping interpretation is that there was no demand for ransom." After a moment's consideration she found another flaw. "Who would ransom her? She has no family. Maxwell mentioned that she is chronically short of funds herself. The only person I can think of is—you." She examined him uncertainly.

"I'm flattered to have become the undisputed focus of your thoughts, Miss Comstock."

"If that's it, you shouldn't have left Belmont."

"If my role is to ransom Fleur, her kidnapper will soon find me."

"Or she'll escape," Pamela added hopefully.

They discussed the case for another few miles, till they had tried all possible combinations of facts, and a good deal of conjecture. The increasing traffic warned them they were approaching London, and their thoughts turned in that direction.

"I hope I find the Fosters at home," Pamela mentioned. "They aren't expecting me till tomorrow." Her relatives were by no means travelers. It was only

111

the possibility of their being out visiting or shopping that she meant.

"I was a little surprised at your coming unannounced a day early."

"I shan't mind if I'm alone with the servants for a few hours, except that I won't be much help to you."

Breslau, long inured to young ladies discovering unlikely excuses for his company, felt no sense of imposition on this occasion. Heartened by her sudden show of interest, he said, "Between the two of us, do you not think we might find an excuse for you not to stay with your Aunt Foster?"

Pamela stared, aghast. "Not stay with her! Breslau, what are you suggesting?"

He realized he had misread her, but having made the suggestion, he played it out. "That you stay with me, in my very well chaperoned house in Belgrave Square. Two maiden aunts are visiting me at the moment."

"How odd it would look! Very singular," she charged, but added more gently, "would it not?"

"Not at all. How are you going to help me find Fleur if you're sequestered in some out-of-the-way house where we can't easily meet and talk?"

Pamela squirmed in discomfort. His plan sounded delightful, but it strained the bounds of propriety. "If I go to Aunt Foster, she won't hear of my not staying with her."

"Then it will be best if you come directly to my house and drop her a note telling her you're in town. We might find a moment to visit her."

"I don't know what Mama would say."

"Are your parents quite set on this match with Nigel?"

"Well," she admitted bluntly, "I am twenty-two years old and have no other parti in sight. It's high time I was bounced off."

Breslau smiled politely. "I'm inclined to agree with you, Pamela. As you said yourself, however, Nigel is scarcely breeched. A few years' seasoning would do him a world of good. You don't mind my calling you Pamela? As you are to visit me, it seems not encroaching. You *do* remember my name? Westbrook, but my friends call me Wes."

"I haven't said I would! I scarcely know you. We only met yesterday."

"True, but already last night you knew me well enough to call me Wes. Do you know me less well today?"

"The strange thing is, I *do* feel I know you less well." She frowned. "I thought you were . . ." She came to a confused pause.

"Do continue. There's nothing I enjoy discussing more than myself."

"That's exactly what I mean! That's the way you seemed yesterday, so horrid and satirical and proud."

"But in England, you must know, we consider pride one of the virtues. An Englishman without his pride is like a sky without a sun."

"Or a dog without fleas. How could a girl possibly—I mean, I didn't even bother trying to—to—"

"I noticed," he said blandly. "My fleas were quite upset that you didn't."

"Didn't what?"

"We both know what you mean, Pamela. Let us not belabor the obvious. Dare I hope your feelings have undergone a change?"

"I'm not sure they have," she said tartly. "The

113

only reason I wanted to come to London with you was because of the marquise, you know."

Breslau patted her fingers. "Cheer up. The excitement isn't over. You may yet have the pleasure of taking the stand at a murder trial."

"I shall now answer a question you asked a moment ago, Lord Breslau. My feelings have not undergone a change where you are concerned. You're as odious as I first thought."

Breslau's playful manner evaporated. The eyes that gazed unblinkingly into hers were serious. "I'm not, you know. I've merely chosen a bad moment for frivolity. It's possible Fleur is in serious trouble, and till we learn the truth, I shan't pester you with any more nonsense."

For a quarter of a mile the only sound was the clatter of the horses jogging along and the running of the carriage wheels. Pamela was almost sorry she'd protested against his playful manner. The silence made it too easy to think, and what she thought was that she shouldn't stay at his house. There was no real excuse for it, yet she felt keenly that the visit would be much more exciting if she stayed with him.

"My Aunt Foster lives on the corner of Half Moon and Curzon streets," she said as the carriage entered London.

Breslau showed her an impassive face. "Is that where you wish me to take you?"

She bit her bottom lip uncertainly. "I really should."

"Last chance," he tempted with a charming smile. "I plan to go to Drury Lane this evening and make enquiries."

"What will you do this afternoon?"

"Go to Fleur's apartment, call on some of her friends, lunch at a little restaurant near the theater. I daresay your Aunt Foster would rather you not accompany me on such outings, though I guarantee no harm would befall you."

Her Aunt Foster would swoon at the very thought of her calling on an actress. Every fiber of her body was eager for the excitement. If she visited her aunt, the best to be hoped for was a visit to some elderly friend, or a drive to Bond Street.

"Well?"

"The Fosters aren't actually expecting me yet," she said.

"Then you must come with me. You wouldn't want to land in on them unannounced. We'll go directly to Belgrave Square. You will want to freshen up before lunch."

A smile of relief broke, and Pamela had difficulty keeping her voice normal. "You're right, of course. It wouldn't do to land in unannounced on my aunt. I'll land in on yours instead. Are they very stiff, Breslau?"

"Where do you think I got this horrid disposition? The whole family is starched daily."

"Then I'm glad we shan't be spending much time with them. What is the restaurant like? Will I see many actors?"

"Mrs. Siddons still drops in from time to time. Would your mama object to your meeting her?"

"Oh, no! Mama is not so bad as Lady Raleigh and Mrs. Foster. She would be thrilled to death. It's Papa who would hit the roof."

All restraint vanished, and the remainder of the trip was highly enjoyable. Lord Breslau had the pleasure of hearing himself called Wes, and the added pleasure of a gasp of surprise when the horses drew up in front of one of the finest mansions in London.

When Pamela spoke, she had trained her voice to nonchalance. Only her staring eyes betrayed her. "Is this where you live?" she asked.

"It is, but as you pointed out, we shan't have to spend much time here. The restaurant is much less pretentious."

Miss Comstock's eyes were as big as saucers, and her heart was thumping in agitation when Lord Breslau took her elbow and escorted her to the front door.

## Chapter Eight

Breslau House was every bit as intimidating as its exterior suggested. After Pamela had been shown to a chamber and refreshed her toilette, she descended to a saloon the size of St. Michael's Church at home. Sofas and seats were ranged around the walls like the waiting room of a superior hotel lobby. Two elderly ladies of forbidding aspect, dressed all in black, sat near the grate. Their heads turned in unison and they stared toward the doorway. Pamela felt an unworthy urge to take to her heels. Suddenly Breslau appeared behind her.

"Stage fright, Miss Comstock?" he teased. "Come now, show your metal. You have an audience of only two, both of whom are eager to be pleased."

That was her salvation. The ladies, pensioners of Lord Breslau's, vied with each other in showering questions and compliments on her. They could conceive of no reason for her visit except that she was Breslau's intended, and were determined to find favor with her.

"From Kent, you say? The flower garden of England," Miss Agatha exclaimed.

"I knew it from your complexion," Miss Anscombe nodded wisely. "Kent gives the finest flowers and complexions."

When the smiles and compliments became excessive, Breslau rescued her. "Miss Comstock is a friend of the Raleighs'. I am delivering her home for them, as I have to go to Kent soon on business."

"I see!" The ladies exchanged a satisfied nod, and damped their enthusiasm down to an acceptable level.

Breslau explained that he and Miss Comstock would not be home for lunch. The aunts expressed a lukewarm interest in having the pleasure of meeting at dinner.

"There, now that wasn't so bad, was it?" he said as they went to the carriage.

"Are they always so effusive?"

"Only when they fear they are meeting my wife-to-be."

"Is that what they thought!" Her amusement was hardly less than her genuine shock.

"You see the danger in associating with an eligible bachelor of good morals."

"Or even one of uncertain moral fiber." She smiled boldly, and to his considerable consternation immediately dropped this promising subject. "Are we going to Fleur's apartment first?"

"My groom went there while we freshened up. Fleur's maid said she's not at home, and hasn't been since leaving for Belmont. We'll drop around after lunch to see if there's been any news."

Pamela found it hard to concentrate on the case when there were so many interesting sights to be seen in the city. Breslau had changed from traveling carriage to city chaise, which bowled along the Strand at a smart pace, passing other elegant carriages. Bows and nods were exchanged through the windows. The ladies' toilettes made Pamela realize that what passed for high style at home was quite inadequate to the job in London.

"I feel like a country mouse," she admitted. "And to think I left my lovely new rose gown at home, hardly worn."

It gave Breslau an excuse to examine her closely. His smile suggested he had no aversion to country creatures, especially when they came with such sparkling eyes. "Why did you not bring it to Belmont?"

"The neck is a little low. Lady Raleigh would have disliked it, but more importantly, Nigel would have approved."

"If that is a hint of shopping trips to come, you must hold me excused. My aunts would be delighted to oblige you, however."

"How can you say so without consulting them?"

"The voice of experience. They are always happy to oblige me, never moreso than when they come uninvited. You see how malleable I am in ladies' hands. It takes very little to turn me up sweet." Breslau was hardly surprised that this leading comment proved unsuccessful in instituting any flirtation. He was coming to know Miss Comstock.

As the carriage turned left into Drury Lane, the setting changed. The street here was a peculiar mixture of the grand and the mean. The courts and blind alleys leading off the main road suggested unabated squalor, yet the street itself was lined with what looked like mansions. The corner buildings in particular were blazing walls of plate glass, bedizened with gilt cornices and bright doorways.

"Gin mills," he explained. This brought a gleam to her eyes. "All the grandeur is on the outside. Our first stop will be the Drury Lane Restaurant on Russell Street, near the theater. Hardly elegant, but better than these dens. Fleur frequents the place. She likes to queen it over her inferiors."

"Speak no ill of the dead, Breslau."

"I hope you like bubble and squeak, and treacle tart for dessert." This sounded entirely appetizing to Pamela.

The carriage soon stopped and Breslau led Miss Comstock into a cheerful café that was abuzz with the animation of actors at leisure. Men with curls hanging over their foreheads and ladies interestingly overdressed were in abundance. No formality whatsoever existed. The inhabitants roamed from table to table for a chat, often carrying a glass or plate with them, eating as they went. Breslau's entrance caused a buzz of excitement. Pamela, too, came in for her share of jealous attention.

They were led to a choice table by the window. "Is Mrs. Siddons here?" she asked, looking around.

The Tragic Muse was not present, but there was plenty to keep Pamela occupied. Before their dinner arrived, a pretty young woman with straw-blond hair and a worried face approached their table.

"You're not supposed to be back till tomorrow, Lord Breslau!" the woman charged.

"As you see, I'm here a day early."

After a moment's hesitation, he decided to present the woman to Pamela. Having brought a lady to such a disreputable place, he could hardly assume a belated air of propriety. The question of why he had brought Pamela nagged at his mind. Was he trying to shock her? To nudge her out of her assumed indifference? Or was it a test of her eligibility to be his wife? A lady who was horrified at the doings of the theater was not the lady for him.

"This is Rose Flanders, Miss Comstock. I believe you're familiar with the name. I'm taking Miss Comstock to see your performance this evening, Rose."

"Oh, you're the actress who is replacing the marquise during her—her holiday," Pamela said, smiling to hide her near lapse.

"Are you an actress?" Rose asked jealously.

"Me?" Pamela exclaimed. "Oh, no."

Rose looked relieved. Breslau cleared his throat and immediately began fishing for information. "Have you seen Fleur around, Rose?"

"Isn't she with you? I hope she ain't planning to take over my role tonight. You said I was to have two nights."

"Fleur isn't with me. You shall have your two nights, as promised. How did it go last night?"

"It was just grand. You could hear the clapping all the way to Covent Garden. But where's Fleur? She said she was going to the country with you and that swell that's writing her life story."

"I had to return to London early. I thought Fleur might have cut the visit short as well. You haven't seen her about then?"

"Not a hair or whisker. Oh, I bet she'll come scrambling back early. Some nosy Parker wrote and warned her what a grand success I was."

As the woman prattled on, Pamela observed her more closely. Rose didn't look a day older than herself. Her gown was a lively red-and-green striped, cut very low in front, but with a shawl that received an occasional tug as a token to propriety. Despite her grammatical lapses and country expressions, Rose spoke with an elegant accent and had a fine, carrying voice.

"Rest assured, tonight is yours," Breslau told her.

This appeared to satisfy Rose, and she joined them for a glass of wine before lunch arrived.

"I'm rather anxious to find Fleur, if she's in town," Breslau said. "She isn't at her apartment."

"She wouldn't be, would she?" Rose said matter-of-factly. "With all her blunt, she'd be out shopping."

"Her servant says she hasn't been home."

"Maybe she went straight to her gentleman friend."

"The general?" Breslau asked.

"That's nought but cream-pot love. She'd never go visiting him—nor would he let her in the door. No, Fleur has a colt's tooth in her head. It's that young Spiedel fellow she goes running to when she has a moment free."

"Would you happen to know where he lives?"

"I saw them slipping into a flat on the corner of Drury Lane and Macklin Street once. I fancy that's where he sleeps."

"Have you seen him around recently?"

"That one is always around. He was loitering backstage last night. He was in the café this morning, but now I think of it, Fleur wouldn't be with him. They had a falling out the last night she was here. I heard a terrific row in her room."

Pamela and Breslau exchanged a meaningful look. "What seemed to be the trouble?" he asked.

"Likely she caught him carrying on with one of the young girls."

While this was interesting, Spiedel had not been at Hatfield, and Breslau soon turned his questions in another direction. "It's possible Spiedel caught Fleur with another man. She's been seeing another young fellow, I think."

"No, has she?" Rose asked eagerly.

"I've seen her speaking to a handsome young lad."

"Henry Halton, you mean?" Rose asked at once.

"A tall, good-looking man. A gentleman, to judge by his appearance. Black hair, slender build."

"That's Henry, handsome as can stare, but the fight wasn't about him. He's seeing Meg Crispin steady now. I can tell you Fleur ain't with him, for he's gone to visit his aunt in the country. She must have sent him a walloping present. Meg says he was hiring a traveling carriage and four horses at Newman's Stables yesterday afternoon."

Pamela nearly choked on her wine. Breslau gave her a quelling look.

"God bless you," Rose said, and gave Pamela a slap on the back. "He's supposed to be back next week, but he won't know nothing about Fleur. What makes you think she left the house party early? She'll stay till the last dog's hung if I know anything. How the gossoon that's writing her story ever got hisself talked into taking her home to meet his ma is more than I know."

"She left early," Breslau insisted.

"Then the lady of the house hinted her away," Rose announced with grim satisfaction.

The food arrived and Rose stood to leave. "Well, nice meeting you, your ladyship." She curtsied to Pamela and left.

"Where did she get the idea I'm a lady? A noble lady, I mean," Pamela added swiftly when a satirical grin tugged at Breslau's lips.

"It must be your lack of conversation that convinced her. You will have noticed that actresses chat more freely."

"Yes, and very much to the point. That argument between Spiedel and Fleur . . ."

"Interesting, but he's been in London all along. Our mysterious stranger must be this Henry Halton—a carriage and team of four, a sudden trip to the country."

"We should have asked where he lives, Wes!"

"I'll have a word with Meg Crispin later. I don't want to arouse too much curiosity in Fleur's activities."

Breslau looked around the room and spotted Meg Crispin at a table with a group of actors. He excused himself, and was soon back with the information, but not before two young fops had sidled up to Pamela's table. Breslau's return sent them packing.

"Halton lives on Wild Street. It's a slum nearby," he said. "Were those yahoos bothering you?"

"Not at all, they were very friendly. We might as well go to Wild Street first."

"That's not a place I can take you. I don't relish the visit myself." He came to a frowning halt. "Why would Halton want to harm Fleur?"

They were interrupted by a young playwright who shoved a bulky manuscript into Breslau's hands with an assurance that he would never have read anything like it, and his address was enclosed.

When the opportunist left, Breslau looked at the dessert menu. "Treacle tart? The apple tart is also fairly edible."

"I'll try the treacle. The bubble and squeak was excellent, by the by."

He smiled approvingly. "Cheap, too. That is the major criterion of the clients here."

"That's a universal criterion."

While they were waiting for dessert, an actor and two actresses came begging for work. Breslau made an appointment to audition them in a week's time.

"I shouldn't think you come here very often, when people pester you so much," she said.

Breslau's ears perked up. Now it was coming! A few animadversions on his life-style. "On the contrary, I come frequently. The moth in me was always attracted to the flame of drama. Coming here feeds my vanity, as well as my stomach."

Her smile was condescending, but it struck her as odd to hear a man speak the unflattering truth about himself so unequivocally. "They seem a very convivial lot," she admitted.

"They're a breed apart; they live for the performance." Breslau's expression assumed an attractive liveliness. "There's an enticing sense of urgency in the life of theater people, and along the way they manage to make all life exciting. Real life lacks that—thrill. I was dozing my life away in the House before I joined the Drury Lane Commission. Now the days aren't long enough to encompass all I must do. Culture is vital to a nation, as vital as politics or wars, or so I have convinced myself. Do you feel no
125

attraction to such a life, even in your more pagan moments?"

"My life has no pagan moments," she said with a definite air of deprivation. Breslau was right. Her life had soared to previously unimagined heights of excitement since meeting Fleur and him. Chatham would be intolerable after this brush with drama. Pamela didn't observe the tense air of expectancy in her companion. Secure that it wouldn't degrade her in his eyes, she told the simple truth. "I adore all this. I wish I could be an actress. Rose Flanders mistook me for one." A pensive smile played over her features.

Breslau was at pains to hide the gloating smile that wanted to come out. Miss Comstock would do. Now he had only to convince her that he would do for her. "Ladies are allowed to play in amateur productions. I plan to try out a new comedy I've written myself. I'll be putting it on at my country estate in the summer. Would you be interested to try your hand in a part?" he asked casually.

She felt a rush of delight, alloyed only by surprise. "Where is your country estate?"

"In Derbyshire."

"That's very far away."

"My carriage will be going, so you needn't worry about your horses being put to the exertion—and the tolls," he added mischievously. A sense of humor was also important in the future Marchioness of Breslau.

She gave him a bantering smile. "That eases my mind considerably, sir. You plutocrats aren't always awake to the inconvenience of not having your pockets full of silver."

"Before you point out the ineligibility of the

scheme, let me say my aunts would be delighted to play propriety."

"I'd have to discuss it with my parents," she said. Her quivering lips and shining eyes spoke clearly of her desire to participate.

"If all else fails," Breslau suggested, "I could invite Nigel along." Her smile faded. He reached for her fingers in an avuncular fashion. "Isn't there always a fly in the ointment?"

"More like a serpent in the Garden of Eden. It sounds heavenly, Breslau."

The treacle tarts arrived and were soon dispatched. Breslau led Pamela to the door amidst a shower of farewells.

"First stop, the corner of Drury Lane and Macklin Street," he called to his driver, and they were off.

The residence was a rambling rooming house, no longer elegant, but not quite sunk below respectability. They read the apartment numbers and climbed up two stories. Breslau tapped on the door and a manservant answered.

"I'd like to see Mr. Spiedel," Breslau said.

"The master's out, sir. Could I tell him who was calling?"

If Spiedel was involved, Breslau didn't want to leave his name. "It's not important. When do you expect him?"

"He comes and goes as he likes."

"Does he dine at home in the evening?"

The man gave him a surly look. "Who's to cook for him? I have enough to do with keeping his boots polished and his clothes in order and the dust and dirt out of the rooms, without turning cook. Mind you I can fry a sausage or a bit of gammon and eggs in a pinch."

"He won't be dining at home, I take it?"

"No, sir, he'll not. Leave a note, if you like."

"I'll come back later. Has Mr. Halton been to call?"

"Who?"

Breslau repeated the name. The servant didn't appear to recognize it, so the guests left, not much wiser than when they arrived. "If Spiedel's in town, he'll turn up at the theater tonight," Pamela said. "In any case, he looks innocent. He doesn't even know Halton. Yet it was Spiedel who argued with Fleur, and Halton who hired the carriage."

"They must have met, at least, as they both hang about the theater. They could be working together."

The marquise's apartment was the next stop. It was situated on the second floor in a respectable brick building on the corner of Upper Grosvenor Square.

"My groom says her maid was at home when he called," Breslau mentioned as they mounted the stairs. "If you could find an excuse into her bedroom, I'll divert Maria while you look for clues. See if she keeps a diary, or has any letters lying around. That sort of thing."

"How can I possibly ask to enter her bedroom?"

"I'm disappointed in you, Pamela. The effectual Miss Comstock stymied by such a detail? You've ripped your sleeve, and wish privacy to mend it. Fleur has only one sitting room, which I shall occupy. This is your opportunity to try your hand at acting."

"All right, I'll do it."

128

When they knocked at Fleur's door, there was no reply.

"The maid must have gone out," Pamela exclaimed.

"That's odd. The reason she didn't accompany Fleur to Belmont was that she had a violent cold. My groom mentioned a racking cough when he was here earlier."

"We really shouldn't disturb her if she's ill. Unless she's so ill that she requires help," Pamela said, looking uncertainly to her companion.

"I'll ask the caretaker to let us inside. He knows me."

A brightly questioning gaze was turned on Breslau. "Do you frequently visit the marquise?"

"That depends on your definition of frequent. Is once a week frequent? When I was wooing her into leaving Covent Garden, I began coming. I still bring a play or song or sketch for a gown around for her consideration from time to time."

"A footman could do that," she snipped.

Breslau felt a sense of gratification at this display of interest that amounted almost to jealousy. "He could, but I like to keep the personal touch with my leading lady. I'll fetch the caretaker."

Pamela was left cooling her heels outside the door till he returned with the key. It annoyed her that Breslau hung on the skirts of such a woman as Fleur. Indeed the whole theater atmosphere, while fascinating, was peopled with too many pretty, friendly actresses to entirely please her.

Breslau returned alone, carrying the key. "Maria's out shopping. A suspiciously rapid recovery."

This didn't strain Pamela's credulity. Once a cold

settled down to a cough, it was only an annoyance. They entered the apartment and she looked around with considerable interest. The drawing room was not only respectable but elegant. There was no garish taste in the gold window hangings or in the dainty striped settee and cut-velvet occasional chairs. The place was small, but well got up. A cursory examination gave no clue as to where the marquise was, or what she was doing.

"The bedroom," Breslau said, and headed for a door.

She noticed he was familiar with the route, and felt a sharper stab of annoyance. She was determined to find the room in bad taste, but had uphill work disparaging such a refined chamber. The canopied bed and window hangings were in a pale green, while the carpet repeated the shade, adding creams and rose. A shower of rosebuds covered the walls. The glowing mahogany furnishings were downscaled to suit a lady's chamber.

"We'll try the desk first," Breslau said, and began sorting through a welter of papers.

Pamela joined him. A silver tray held an oddment of letters, invitations, bills, and theater sheets. Breslau rifled through them and removed the letters.

"You're not going to read her private correspondence!"

"How else are we going to learn what she's up to?"

"It seems horrid."

"Fleur is in trouble, Pamela. We have to find her."

With this reason for doing what she very much wished to do, Pamela, too, began opening envelopes and glancing through letters. There were several from gentlemen trying to arrange an introduction.

She mentioned the names to Breslau, who shook his head. "It's Max, Spiedel, and Henry Halton we're interested in. Or anything bearing a crest."

The only item of interest was some correspondence from J. Spiedel. He was a frequent writer, and obviously a frequent guest as well. Several notes expressed thanks for the charming dinner the evening before. Others suggested rendezvous in secluded spots. More than one thanked Fleur for her "generosity."

"Does he mean money, or—" Pamela came to an embarrassed halt.

After enjoying her discomfiture for a moment, he said, "There's no tone of the lover. On the other hand, I don't see why she'd continuously give blunt to a young hanger-on she's not involved with. Fleur's not clutchfisted, but she likes value for her money."

Pamela glanced at another note. "It's money," she said. "Ten pounds. He's telling her he ordered the new jacket, and will present himself at the theater for her approval. What a parasite." She read on. "Now he's dunning Fleur for an acting job in one of her plays. How interesting. 'You can always bring Lord Breslau around your thumb!' How is this winding job achieved, Breslau?"

He threw up his shoulders. "I've already told you; I am putty in the hands of a beautiful woman."

After one scathing glance, Pamela continued the letter, which was longer than most. "It seems Mr. Spiedel is less malleable. 'Pray do not bother using your influence to get me any position as a scribbler for an M.P. It would not suit me at all. I have told you so more than once.' Pretty cheeky!"

"Fleur never asked me to hire Spiedel."

"So I gathered, or he'd be treading the boards. What's that you've got there?"

"Her bank statement."

"She must be broke, supporting Spiedel and herself."

"On the contrary, she's high in the stirrups."

Pamela went to his shoulder to see for herself. "Those three large deposits over the past six months—they would be benefit performances, or something of the sort?"

"No. Benefits are usually performed for ill or retiring actors. This isn't money from her acting."

"I daresay she has investments in Consols that pay her interest."

"That's possible," he said.

"She's rich as Croesus! A quarterly interest of a thousand pounds indicates an extremely large amount of capital, something in the order of eighty thousand pounds," Pamela said, frowning over the figures. "The only other thing I can think of is—" She stopped.

"It looks that way. She's blackmailing someone."

"I didn't mean that!"

"Did you not, Miss Comstock? Then you obviously imply she has a keeper. I've noticed your mind has a tendency to dwell on illicit affairs. Shocking, and you a country-bred girl."

"That is not restricted to the city I assure you."

"True, making love appears to be a universal vice."

"And my mind does not *dwell* on it."

"You're right. Harp is the word I should have used. Your mind *does* digress to more edifying matters—murder, turning actress. There's nothing more to be learned here. Mr. Halton's residence is the next stop. Would you like to take this opportunity to visit your Aunt Foster?"

"Very well. Of course she'll expect me to stay if I go in person," she added with a quick peep to read his reaction.

Breslau looked perfectly indifferent, but his words cheered her. "Then you would prefer to go to Belgrave Square and write her a note."

"If you're asking my preference, I would prefer to go to Wild Street."

"Ladies always do enjoy a brush with lowlife, but you've had quite enough enjoyment for one day. And incidentally, when you speak to Aunt Agatha, we haven't been to the Drury Lane Restaurant."

"Have we not been here, either, calling on Fleur?"

"Fleur who?" he asked, and took her arm to lead her downstairs.

A gurgle of laughter rose in her throat. "And I thought you were so toplofty! You're a fraud, Lord Breslau."

His attempt at showing offense failed miserably. A boyish grin removed the last trace of arrogance from his refined features, rendering him much more attractive to his companion. "Appearing bored with my calling lightens the odium of it, in the eyes of my family and their more dignified friends. Now that you have joined my circle of *intîmes*, Pamela, there is no need for me to sham it with you."

"Well that's a relief. And now that I am an *intîme*, may I go with you to Wild Street?"

He raised a thin finger. "There is where you misread me. I may do all the slumming I like, and enjoy it thoroughly. You, on the other hand, being a

133

maiden of unsullied reputation, must tow the line. Till a lady has nabbed herself an unexceptionable parti, she must be above reproach, like Caesar's wife."

"I doubt that you would have taken Calpurnia to the Drury Lane Restaurant to dine on bubble and squeak."

"Not while Caesar was in charge of the Roman army, certainly. If you wish to continue this depraved existence, you must heed my warning—the one about nabbing an unexceptionable husband."

"A high price to pay for a visit to a slum."

"This is true," he agreed, and laughed.

Pamela was returned to Breslau House and dutifully wrote up her letter to the Fosters. She refrained from writing to Harley, as he would certainly come pelting to Belgrave Square immediately. She spent a tiresome thirty minutes in front of the grate with Breslau's aunts, inventing a polite lunch and drive to account for the time less genteelly occupied. As afternoon shadows turned the saloon to a cave, Breslau returned. He wore his toplofty mask, for his aunts' benefit.

Pamela assumed the aunts wouldn't recognize the name and said, "Did you find your friend, Mr. Halton, at home, Breslau?"

"Unfortunately Henry left town and hasn't returned yet. Even his servants were out. A neighbor told me he was away."

"No word when he might return?"

"I'm afraid not."

They exchanged a worried, questioning look. "It's rather chilly. I believe I'll get my shawl," Pamela said, and left the room, looking over her shoulder for Breslau to follow her.

He rose almost at once. "I'll freshen up for dinner now. Would you please hurry dinner forward tonight, Aunt Agatha? I'm in a bit of a rush."

Pamela was waiting for him at the bottom of the stairs. "What have you been doing all afternoon?" he asked.

"Gathering dust with your maiden aunts."

"You have me back now. I hang on your lightest word. Those speaking eyes suggest you want to quiz me."

"Did you go back to Spiedel's flat?"

"There and to the theater. I kept missing him by minutes, but he's around town."

"I wonder what he and Fleur argued about."

Breslau looked distracted. "I'd like to know who she was getting money from. Neither Spiedel nor Halton has two pence to rub together. She couldn't be blackmailing them."

"We have no proof she's blackmailing anyone."

"You're harping again, Pamela."

"There are other ways of making money!"

"The marquise is not a doctor or lawyer or financier. If you actually have a sensible idea, I'd like to hear it."

"Nigel mentioned the Frenchies had asked her to spy for them."

Breslau brushed it aside. "I said sensible. Fleur has no state secrets to sell. She isn't interested in politics."

"What other sort of secrets could she have, that she can hold someone to ransom? Who could she be blackmailing?"

"Any one of her ex-lovers who has attained a position of importance. It begins to look as if her victim tired of paying up and decided to—terminate the arrangement."

"Terminate Fleur, you mean?"

"That would be the surest way of doing it."

Pamela's heart clenched and her head felt light. "You really think she's dead?"

It was impossible to read Breslau's expression. He didn't look as worried as he should if he thought Fleur was dead. Yet he was genuinely concerned. Pamela felt her own anxiety shrink, but it didn't dissipate.

"I'm afraid we have to consider that possibility. We'll go to the theater tonight as planned. I want to ask some questions backstage. Rose might know something. She mentioned Fleur having a deal of money. I thought at the time it was only a dig at the difference in their salary. Perhaps she meant more than that. She might have some ideas regarding the source of all this money."

"We still haven't spoken to Spiedel. He was on such close terms with Fleur that he might know something—if he's not the culprit himself, that is."

"If he's not at the theater, I'll slip back to his apartment during the play."

"You seem really worried, Wes."

He rubbed his chin with his knuckles. "I am, rather."

Chapter Nine

In retrospect, it seemed to Pamela that where Breslau made his mistake was in returning home for dinner. If they had not done so—and the meal was tediously formal—his aunts would not have taken the idea to accompany them to the play. It was small consolation that the aunts nodded approval of her plain blue gown. Even Breslau's moderate compliment that he couldn't imagine why she so strongly preferred the rose left at home didn't satisfy her. She knew when she was seated between Miss Agatha and Miss Anscombe in his box that the only excitement she might expect from the evening was the drama on stage.

Of course it was a thrill to be seated on the grand tier, the butt of much curiosity from the bejeweled ladies and dashing gentlemen inhabiting the other boxes. Rose played her role of Emily in *The Deuce Is in Him* with verve and style, but throughout the first act Pamela kept waiting for it to be over, so that she might go backstage with Breslau.

Her hopes were dashed entirely. At the intermission, Breslau leaned across to his Aunt Agatha and explained that he must leave for a moment, but would have wine sent in. When Pamela rose to join him, Agatha put a bony hand on her arm and said, "There is no need to disturb yourself, Miss Comstock. You would not want to meet the rakes and rattles who prowl the corridors at intermission. You will be better off here, with us."

Pamela cast a demanding eye on Breslau, and discovered a smile lurking on his lips. "Quite right," he agreed.

"Beast!" she hissed as he took his leave.

"I'll give you all the details after the play."

She had no opportunity to revile him till the next intermission, when she claimed her legs were cramped and, despite the low company prowling the corridors, she really *must* have a little stroll.

"Try if you can find a quiet hallway, Breslau," Miss Agatha advised with a sorry shake of her head.

As soon as they were out of the box, Pamela turned a wrathful eye on him. "You did it on purpose! Don't bother denying it. In fact, you invited your aunts to join us. Why did you tell them we were coming to Drury Lane?"

"I had to. They had the tickets."

"You could have told them you'd given the extra seats in the box to someone else."

"You would urge me to lie, Miss Comstock?" he *tsk*'d. "What next?"

"You lie as quick as a dog would trot. You've told a dozen plumpers since we got to London. Did you not instruct me to let on my gown was ripped, so you could read Fleur's private correspondence?"

"Now do you feel better?" he asked with a show

of solicitude. "Aunt Agatha was quite right, for once. My destination was the greenroom, you see."

"But I should *love* to visit a greenroom, of all things!"

"Like is drawn to like, greenhead to greenroom. I made sure you'd employ these few moments to ask what I learned."

"Did you hear something?" she asked eagerly.

"Spiedel's there, tearing his hair and buttonholing everyone, including the handymen, to ask what they've done with the marquise. If the lad is acting, I mean to hand him the lead in the next play whether Fleur likes it or not. Actually it may be too late for that now. Rose tells me he's been offered a minor role at Covent Garden. She thinks that is what his argument with Fleur was about."

"That hardly sounds fatal. And he doesn't know where she is?"

"I'm convinced of it. He was close to tears. 'She was an angel, and I was constantly displeasing her. She didn't ask much of me, and she was so generous. I should have done what she wanted.' That sort of carry on."

"What did she want him to do?"

"Refuse the role at Convent Garden, I expect. Rose and the others are becoming mighty curious. We can't keep Fleur's disappearance a secret much longer. We have either to find her or call in the police."

"Why do you say disappearance, Breslau? Would *murder* not be the more appropriate word?"

"We shan't know that till we find her, or her body."

"I assume Henry Halton wasn't there, or you would have told me."

"No. His lady, Meg Crispin, had a letter delivered

by a messenger claiming he'd been delayed a few days in Kent. It didn't come by post, if that means anything."

Pamela considered this. "He went to Hatfield, not Kent. Why is he lying if he's not up to something?"

"He'd have no reason to lie to Meg. Perhaps he *is* in Kent. The flaw in choosing Halton for the villain is that he has no money, and he's too young to have a history worthy of blackmail. Of course he could be acting for someone else."

"You always keep harping on blackmail."

"How else can we account for her having Lady Raleigh's diamond bracelet?"

They discussed this for a few moments. When the warning bell rang, they turned back toward their box. "I wonder when we can expect to see General Max," Pamela said.

"If he's not here by morning, I'll return to Belmont. Will you come with me, or shall I take you to your Aunt Foster's? Tomorrow is the day you were supposed to join her."

Neither destination pleased Miss Comstock. She wanted to remain exactly where she was. She wanted the crime to come to her, but as this was impossible, she asked, "When do you expect to come back to London?"

Breslau's eyebrow lifted in a question. "As soon as possible, *ça va sans dire.* Do I detect a note of eagerness for my return?"

"Of course. If you knew how dull it is at Fosters', you'd understand my reluctance to go there. But I may as well stay in London. It will look odd if I return to Belmont uninvited."

The eyebrow settled down to its usual ennui. During the remainder of the performance, Breslau pondered whether Miss Comstock didn't know how to flirt, or was purposely refusing to oblige him. Or was she more subtle than he supposed? Was her ignoring of all his leading sallies itself not a sort of inverse flirtation? It certainly piqued his interest. While he considered this matter, his eyes often turned to examine her for clues. She had a charming profile, but not once during the last act did she turn to face him head on. That was carrying inverse flirtation too far to please him.

Breslau's offer to take the ladies to the Pulteney for dinner after the play was brushed aside by his aunts before Pamela could express her delight. "It is pretty late already, Breslau. I haven't been up so late since the last time you lured me into visiting Drury Lane. Meat sits like lead on the stomach in the evening and agitates the bile. We would all be better satisfied with a nice cup of hot gruel at home before bed. Your cook makes an excellent gruel."

The making of an excellent gruel was the subject during the drive home. Miss Agatha was in favor of a lemon rind to flavor the groats. Miss Anscombe would hear of nothing but nutmeg. Breslau was called on to settle the matter, and confounded them both by insisting that sherry was the only additive allowed.

"We always use port at home," Pamela said.

"Port!" Three outraged voices came at her in the carriage.

"Port," she insisted, for she was feeling cross after her frustrating evening.

As soon as her gruel was drunk, Pamela made her curtsies and left. There had been no further opportunity for private conversation with Breslau. Miss Agatha and Miss Anscombe admitted, after they had retired, that they were not unhappy to learn Miss Comstock was only a friend of Breslau's. A little forthcoming, leaving the box at the second intermission. One of those clamorous ladies who must always be doing. The greater crime was adding port to the gruel, though it had not destroyed their snack as utterly as they had feared.

Breslau went to his study and sat on alone at his desk, sipping sherry while his gruel turned cold in the cup. He took up a pen and began toying with it. Fleur had been gone for twenty-four hours. Disappeared bag and baggage from a thoroughly respectable house to which she had gone with the intention of showing General Max she was socially acceptable. Was she really naive enough to think one visit at a decent home would do it?

She had gone without her maid, who, if she had ever been ill, had recovered with suspicious celerity. Of course the presence of a second party would have made kidnapping a trifle awkward. There had been no ransom note. Fleur, with her love of costumes, had only taken two gowns with her, one for day wear and one for evening.

Another question rose up to bother him. Where was Fleur's butler during all this? He hadn't gone to Belmont, and there was no sign of him at the apartment. Of course Fleur might have given him a few days off. When a man hired a carriage and team of four, he required a driver, unless he was accomplished enough with the reins to handle four horses himself. Halton had not hired a driver. The rig had been delivered to his apartment and the driver returned to Newman's. Fleur's butler acted as John Groom on those occasions when she bothered to hire job horses for her rig.

He had seen enough of the memoirs to know they were innocent to the point of dullness. Her erstwhile lovers had nothing to fear on that score. Unless she was writing to them, hinting that the book could be altered ... If that was what she was up to, she'd chosen a deuced bad time for it, just when she was trying to rope Maxwell into a proposal. Even without those large, irregular deposits, Fleur was by no means poor. Few men made thirty guineas a day, and outside of her toilette, she wasn't a big spender.

Spiedel couldn't say enough good of her. "So generous," he said more than once, but the generosity seemed to amount to an occasional dinner and a jacket. What the lad really wanted was a role in one of her plays. That would have cost her nothing and ensured Spiedel's society, but she adamantly refused to help. So far from helping, she had bluntly told him not to hire Spiedel. Was she afraid Rose or one of the younger girls would steal him? He'd be snapped up in two minutes by one of the Covent Garden belles. But if she was planning to marry Maxwell, she wouldn't expect to keep Spiedel on the string.

"If you want to help the boy, get him a position at Whitehall. You must know some cabinet minister who needs a secretary. I don't want Spiedel on the stage with me. He's too young and too pretty. He would make me look a hag," she had said.

How old was Fleur? She'd been acting at the Comédie Française at the time of the Revolution. She must have been at least—say, sixteen, seventeen?— at the time. He began jotting down dates and ciphering. That would put her in the upper thirty's now. Well preserved, of course—from the stage she looked at least a decade younger. The memoirs hinted at an unlikely thirteen or fourteen at the time of her arrival at Brighton in 1790, twenty-two years ago. The marriage to the Marquis de Chamaude was called an arranged marriage. Breslau considered it an imaginary marriage. There was no longer a noble Chamaude family in the French book of peerages.

Why bother claiming a husband? Was it a hankering for a title? Did she come encumbered with a child, perhaps . . . His pen hovered over what he had written. Twenty-two years ago. Any child she'd had would be grown up now. A young man, or woman. The words *your son* echoed in his head. Fleur had said them in a loud, angry voice at Belmont. Nigel was the right age, but that was mere meandering. Lady Raleigh had given birth to Nigel herself. Anyone who was interested might hear the story of her confinement, with the heedless Aubrey off at Brighton amusing himself at the Prince's pavilion. The hairs on the back of Breslau's neck began to lift in inspiration.

He sipped the sherry slowly, his eyes narrowed in thought. Yes, that would account for wanting money she didn't need for herself. It would account for those unexplained deposits in her bank, and for Sir Aubrey giving her the bracelet. It wasn't perfectly clear why she had played dead for Nigel, but no doubt his interruption was extremely untimely. Her disappearance had brought Maxwell and Spiedel to heel very nicely. Was it possible he, himself, was also expected to accede to her ridiculous demands?

If he guessed aright, it would account for Halton's

hiring the carriage, for the maid's convenient cold, and for Fleur's disappearance from Belmont. It would even account for Halton's being in Kent. A sardonic grin tugged at his lips. Oh, yes, and for General Max's glove and her own new "old favorite" shawl. Fleur was really up to all the rigs. Turning the badger sett into her grave was a master stroke. One such clever stroke deserved another.

He drew out four sheets of paper and wrote up notices for all the morning papers, called a footman, and had them delivered that night, with a special request that they should appear in the morning's paper in a prominent position.

In the morning, Pamela went to her room to repack her bags for the remove to Fosters' after breakfast. She had scarcely spoken to Breslau. He had his head buried in the papers. He would want an early start to Belmont, and she had no wish to spend the day with Miss Anscombe and Miss Agatha. When she came downstairs to say her farewells, she discovered company had arrived.

"Some gentlemen called for Breslau," Miss Agatha said. "He's in the study with them now. I believe you are acquainted with the callers, Miss Comstock. He mentioned a Mr. Raleigh."

"Nigel?"

"Mr. Raleigh was the name," Miss Agatha informed her with a supercilious lift of her brow.

"Excellent!" Pamela exclaimed, and darted off without so much as a by your leave.

Miss Agatha's cocked ear heard perfectly well that the chit didn't even knock on the door, but just

145

barged into Breslau's study unannounced. Country manners!

It was General Maxwell who held the floor when Pamela arrived on the scene. His blustering voice told her he had learned something, and Nigel's scowl informed her that whatever it was, he didn't like it.

"I shall go directly to Bow Street and inform the authorities," Maxwell announced.

"Let us go through it once more before you do anything rash, General," Breslau said calmly.

Pamela edged closer to Nigel and demanded an explanation. While Maxwell blustered and Breslau tried to calm him, Nigel told the story.

"The foolishest thing you ever heard. Maxwell has taken the absurd idea that Papa had something to do with it. Just because he found his raincoat hidden in the bushes, and a pair of galoshes all covered in mud. He says it's the same sort of mud we have at the badger sett. Mud is mud, if you want my opinion. Anyone might have worn them for that matter. They were always left in the vestibule at the back door."

"But he found them in the bushes? Which bushes?"

"That hedge around the garden outside Fleur's apartment. As if Papa would be fool enough to leave them there if he *had* worn them, which he didn't. We know pretty well whose glove was found in the grave."

General Maxwell overheard this charge, stated in a loud voice for that purpose.

"I can only think of one person who might have stolen my glove!" Maxwell retorted. "You were always hanging around me and Fleur. You took it to cast suspicion on me. If it wasn't your father, it was you who did it, jackanapes. You've been dangling at her skirt tails the past month, casting your puppy eyes on her."

"That's better than old goat's eyes!" Nigel shouted.

Breslau let them go to it. He wanted a minute to collect his thoughts. He had seen Sir Aubrey slipping away from Fleur's room the night of her disappearance, but he hadn't been carrying her clothes away to dispose of them. Neither did he show any signs of having been outdoors. Breslau thought his errand there had to do with the bracelet, perhaps wanting it back in exchange for a promissory note.

"What does Sir Aubrey say?" he asked during the first lull in the argument.

"Naturally he claims to know nothing about it," General Maxwell replied. His tone showed his opinion of this.

"Did you discover anything about the carriage and team of four you were supposed to look into?" Breslau asked.

"It stopped at the George, as you told us. There was only one groom."

"Did you get a description of him?"

"He never opened his mouth. A silent, surly brute."

"But his size, his age?"

"Raleigh wouldn't use his own groom," General Maxwell pointed out, which brought Nigel's clenched fists up, and caused him to hop around in a bad imitation of a bruiser.

The general ignored this blustering charade. "Mrs. Bell and a few other old cats from Hatfield saw it heading toward Belmont around midnight," he continued.

"It wasn't, by any chance, seen headed south toward Kent at a later hour?" Breslau asked hopefully.

"No one saw it again after that. It disappeared. Did it ever reach London, I wonder?"

"It didn't," Breslau said. "I had my groom run over to Newman's Stables and enquire. It isn't slated to return for a few days." He explained who had hired the carriage. The name of Henry Halton wasn't familiar to Maxwell, though he repeated recognizing that sly face at the assembly. Nigel thought he'd heard the name somewhere or other.

"I daresay Sir Aubrey would recognize the name!" General Maxwell said with another fuming look at Nigel.

"If you're looking for a duel, old man, you need look no further."

"That is an honor reserved for equals, not puppies."

Nigel rose like a fish to the fly.

"Cut line," Breslau said curtly. "We're getting nowhere with this bickering. A few new points have come up here in London."

"Who are you calling a puppy?" Nigel demanded. "Whelp!"

Breslau looked at Pamela, shrugged his shoulders and said, "Lead the pup away, if you can. I want a word with the old goat."

She put her hand on Nigel's elbow and spoke quietly. "You must be fatigued and famished after the trip. Let us go into the morning room for some tea. I'll tell you what we've been doing here."

This struck him as a good idea. The general's carriage was as hard sprung as a hay wagon, and the old fool pushed his prads along at a merciless pace. "I'll be back, sir," he told Maxwell, then he left at a stiff-legged gait. Maxwell reached for the sword that used to hang at his side in the good old days. Finding only his pocket, he pulled out a handkerchief and blew his nose instead.

"The nerve of that old bleater, trying to blame it on Papa!" Nigel complained when they were out of the room.

To calm him, Pamela said, "Anyone could have worn the raincoat and galoshes. For that matter, Fleur could have worn them herself. To protect her sable and slippers, you know." The teapot was still on the table and she poured two cups.

"Yes, but as she never came back, she couldn't be the one who hid them in the bushes. How did Maxwell happen to find them if he didn't know they were there?" he asked sagely. "He slipped in that open door and killed her, Pam. Poor Fleur, she must have left the door open for him. She was already dead the first time I went to her room."

"Perhaps she had been out. That would account for the cold arms."

"She wasn't wet, and it was raining."

"She could have worn your father's coat and galoshes."

"What would she do that for?"

"To protect her clothes if she was going to meet someone."

Nigel pulled at his ear, frowning. He had been reviewing every word Fleur had uttered at Belmont, and one speech bothered him. How had she known his papa raised sheep? He certainly hadn't discussed farming with her, though she said he had. Mama

149

had noticed something suspicious, too. She had gone to Fleur's room before dinner, and she hadn't answered the door. Fleur couldn't have fallen asleep in two minutes in the middle of the afternoon, so where was she? Had she gone for a walk and come across the sheep field? Fleur didn't walk just for the fun of it. If she went out, she was certainly meeting someone. Meeting the person in a field isolated from the house suggested some havey-cavey business.

It seemed possible to discuss it with Pamela, who was being unusually understanding today. She listened quietly, but could make nothing of it. Nigel was soon back on his hobbyhorse of blaming Maxwell.

"He was hiding in the closet when I found her the first time, and carried her off as soon as I left."

"Why would he do that?"

"To hide the body in the badger sett. Wes says there's no case without a body, you know. Then he slipped back in and took away her clothes to make us think she'd left willingly."

"The other carriage was waiting near the spinney."

"Maxwell is the only one who saw it lurking by the spinney. I don't have to tell you what *his* evidence is worth. The others only saw a carriage on the road. Nothing in that. What would you expect to see on a public road except carriages?"

"I wonder why Breslau asked if it was headed toward Kent?"

"Very likely he's trying to implicate you." Nigel realized he had strayed from his chosen path of blaming Maxwell and asked, "What have you and Wes been doing here?"

She outlined their discoveries.

"Maxwell obviously hired Henry Halton to give him a hand. That's why he's letting on he don't know him," Nigel decided. "When Halton gets back, I'll beat him till he tells me where they put her body."

"Breslau thinks blackmail may be involved."

"It wouldn't surprise me a bit if she had something on Maxwell. Not that she'd ever stoop so low as to blackmail anyone."

"I don't think it was Maxwell he had in mind."

Nigel bristled up fiercely. "If you're saying that diamond bracelet was blackmail, Pamela—"

"No, no," she assured him. "But why did your papa give it to her?"

"How should I know? A son can hardly ask his father such a thing. Maybe she bought it from him. Mama never wears it. Fleur is very fond of diamonds, and Papa is worried about money just now. I've seen him pouring over his account books. It's just the sort of thing she'd do, to help out a friend."

"Of course." Pamela didn't betray her opinion of this foolishness by so much as a blink. "I never thought of that."

"Well, you don't know Fleur as I do," he said forgivingly.

The day's excitement lent a sparkle to Pamela's eyes and a becoming flush to her cheeks. In honor of London, she had her hair carefully arranged in a new do seen at the theater the night before. She looked much prettier than usual, and her behavior today had been exactly what a man would want—very meek and reasonable. Nigel looked at her with the dawning of a new interest. Pamela wouldn't be half bad if she'd only stay like this.

151

It was his blighted love for Fleur that added the final touch of magic. Fleur was unique, of course. There wasn't such another woman in the world, but besides being too old for him, he had come to realize she wasn't quite the thing. Just a touch fast, leaving her door open to welcome that old goat of a Maxwell into her room, and under his father's roof. Really, that was coming it a bit strong. One would be better off with a genuine lady, like Pam. He could leave her at Belmont with the kids while he followed his career in London. A man had to have legitimate heirs after all.

What was passing in Breslau's study they had no idea. Pamela assumed Wes was relating their findings; Nigel knew Maxwell was trying to poison Wes's mind with lies about his father. Wes wouldn't be fool enough to listen to that poppycock. Wes would decide what was to be done.

It was half an hour before they were called back into the study to hear his decision. Pamela stood dumbfounded when he announced it.

"General Maxwell agrees with me that we should do nothing further for the moment. He and Nigel will be remaining in London."

"Breslau! Aren't you going to try to find Fleur's murderer?" Pamela demanded.

"We have found him," Nigel said with a challenging eye at the general. "And if you don't call in Bow Street, Wes, I shall."

"That won't be necessary," Breslau said blandly. "Nor would your papa thank you for doing anything so woolly-headed, Nigel. Just sit tight."

Nigel ranted wildly about the room. "I never thought you was such a flat, Breslau. You've let this old war-horse convince you he's innocent, when anyone with half an eye in his head can see he's as guilty as sin."

Maxwell just shook his head. His tolerant smile was enough to infuriate a saint, and enough to give Nigel second thoughts. There was something deep going on here. Old Max wouldn't be smiling like a horse trader if it wasn't something that reflected badly on Papa. Perhaps he'd best say nothing till he got Wes alone and heard the whole story.

"We should be trying to locate Halton and the carriage he hired, at least," Pamela suggested.

"It will be back before nightfall," Breslau told her.

"Nightfall! That's hours away!"

"So it is. Why don't you have Nigel take you shopping? I have some errands to perform. I'm sure you will want a few new gewgaws for the theater tonight."

"We were at Drury Lane last night," she reminded him.

"The more interesting melodrama will take place backstage tonight."

Nigel and Pamela exchanged a bewildered look. Nigel leaned closer and said in a low voice, "He's finally done it. Gone completely crazy. It's up to us to find out what the deuce is going on here, Pam. We'll humor him, and pretend we're going shopping. I have a few things we must look into."

Pamela wasn't convinced the wily gleam in Breslau's eye denoted insanity. Far from it. She was on thorns to learn what he knew.

"I'll just get my bonnet and pelisse," she said, and hurried after Breslau when he left to have the carriage summoned. As soon as the butler left, she snatched at his arm. "What are you up to?" she demanded, all formality abandoned.

He looked at her hand, then looked at Pamela. Something in his eyes made her loosen her hold. "Is that why you came chasing after me?" he asked. As she watched, his face softened, and his thin lips parted in a small smile. "I made sure it was to thank me for rescuing you from the Fosters."

"Out of the frying pan, into the fire. You've saddled me with Nigel for the whole day."

"You might take this opportunity to divest yourself of his attentions once and for all."

"That's hardly my top priority at a time like this."

Breslau took hold of her hand and stepped into the closest doorway, which happened to be the butler's room, out of view of any observers. Without releasing her hand, his other arm went around her waist "It is precisely 'at a time like this' that your being Nigel's intended is intolerable," he said in a hushed voice.

Pamela was stunned, as if he'd struck her. "What on earth are you doing?" she gasped.

"Shocking the unshockable Miss Comstock, it seems." He smiled, and placed a light kiss on her cheek.

"You're trying to divert me with this tasteless flirtation," she decided, and was at pains to conceal how well he was succeeding.

"You *are* familiar with the *word* then, if not the deed?" he asked archly.

Her heart hammered irregularly. Her cheek felt scalded where his lips had touched it. She made a token effort to free herself, and was considerably diverted when he refused to release her. Instead he put

154

his other arm around her, but loosely. She hardly felt free to accuse him of holding her prisoner.

"I obviously lack your close familiarity with the deed."

"Till now you've lacked a competent instructor"— he smiled—"but diverting you from too close a questioning is only a secondary motive in this tasteless performance. Are you not interested in my primary one?" His eyes lingered meaningfully on her lips.

She stared steadfastly into the distance. "No," she said firmly.

A quiet laugh echoed in the room. "Stubborn to the last gasp, Miss Comstock. And here you assured me you were no actress."

"I am only interested in what you and General Maxwell plan to do. You might as well tell me, Breslau, or you'll have Nigel and myself on your tail all day."

He shook his head confidently. "We'll lose you before we hit the Strand. Max and I shall be using my team and carriage, you see. Enjoy your day." On that maddening speech he finally released her.

"You *are* a beast!"

Breslau considered her charge a moment. "This is true," he nodded. "Broadly speaking, life on the planet is composed of flora and fauna. I am certainly no flower."

"An *affected* beast. Why do you say 'this' when you mean 'that'?"

"A vulgar wish to be noticed. Let us not splice hairs, my pet. Both are demonstrative pronouns. I maintain that when I do *this*"—he lifted her fingers and placed a light kiss on her knuckles—"I am demonstrating an interest in a beautiful young lady. And when I do *that*"—he turned her hand over and placed a kiss in her palm—"I demonstrate precisely the same thing." He lifted his eyes, which danced with mischief. "Don't you agree, Miss Comstock?"

She slowly withdrew her hand. Both demonstrations affected her most forcefully. Her palm tingled from his kiss, and her voice was breathless. "I never heard such sophistry," she breathed.

"Brace yourself to hear worse this evening," he threatened. "I do admit, however, that you have some cause for annoyance, so I'll give you a clue regarding the new development in the case."

Her eyes shone with interest, and her lips parted in a smile. Watching her, Breslau made a spontaneous motion toward her, but froze when she stepped back.

"The clue?" she asked.

"Wretch! You'll find it on the entertainment page of the *Morning Observer*. It's placed in a black box for maximum visibility. It should keep you busy and out of mischief."

"Reading a notice in the paper won't take all day. How am I to get in the rest of the time?"

"Make yourself at home. Pick up a rag and dust off Aunt Agatha."

On this cavalier speech he strode from the room to take up his curled beaver, overcoat, and gloves. General Maxwell joined him and the two of them left.

Nigel strolled into the hallway. "Did you discover where they're going?" he asked.

"The *Morning Observer*!" she exclaimed, and darted off to the morning room.

# Chapter Ten

The whole front page of the *Morning Observer* was taken up with articles relating to the Prince of Wales's appointment as Regent pending the King's indisposition. This news was a few weeks old, but every day added more details to the appointment. Pamela spent very little time scanning the columns. The Regent would keep his father's ministers in office. Whigs throughout the country read it with stunned disbelief, but it brought only a fleeting frown of impatience to Pamela. That he refused to open parliament in person didn't even merit a frown. This was not what Breslau was referring to.

She turned the page and gave a gasp of surprise. FLAWLESS FLEUR MISSING, BELIEVED DEAD was printed in heavy black type. How had the papers learned of it? With Nigel looking over her shoulder, she read avidly.

The Marquise de Chamaude, famed Drury Lane actress, had disappeared from the home of Sir A. and Lady——, where she had gone to spend a two-day holiday. The following paragraphs were familiar, having to do with escaping Paris in a cart of cabbages and eventually landing at Brighton, to be rescued by the prince.

The rest of the highly colored account was wildly inaccurate. About the only word of truth in it was that the marquise's memoirs would soon be published by Colchester Press. Nigel frowned to see the editor's name had been omitted entirely. They read with considerable surprise that the marquise had been troubled prior to and during her country visit. The intimation was that French spies were after her, and she had fled to the country to escape death. But death may have found her. She had been carried off from her bed while sleeping.

The writer concentrated on the grave—no mention of its being a badger sett—and the marquise's favorite shawl. He omitted that a glove had been found as well. An illustrator had drawn the grave in the middle of a graveyard, surrounded by mourning yews and headstones. With artistic liberty, he sketched in a corpse covered with a paisley shawl.

A few paragraphs gave a resumé of Fleur's most popular roles, and a tantalizing hint that her life story was already being dramatized for Drury Lane. It was suggested that Rose Flanders, the marquise's understudy and a talented performer in her own right, might play the role. "Tasteless!" Pamela frowned. The final item was a lugubrious question—would the Flawless Fleur be found alive? They read it twice, wondering aloud who had informed the papers.

"Breslau will be furious," Nigel said.

"He didn't seem furious. In fact, he was smiling while he was reading this at breakfast."

"Was he, by Jove. It'd be the free publicity that

cheered him. I hope no one knows Sir A. and Lady —— are Mama and Papa. They will be far from smiling, I promise you."

"Since your name is not mentioned no one will know who is meant. What bothers me is how the journals got the story. You don't think—"

"That Breslau sent it in? It looks suspicious when you count up how often the words Drury Lane crop up. This will fill the seats."

"No, it's just that the words about her escaping from France are almost exactly as she said them to me at Belmont. Except that Fleur knew it was rutabagas in the cart, not cabbages."

"It's taken word for word from her memoirs, and any number of people have read them. How could Fleur have sent it in? She's dead."

"We don't know that. Breslau doesn't believe it. He isn't worried enough. Maxwell is genuinely disturbed, though."

"Of course he is. He'll be doing the hangman's jig once I get all this figured out. I shouldn't be a bit surprised if he put Fleur up to gouging that diamond bracelet out of Papa to incriminate him. If I could find the bracelet in his possession, that would tell us something."

"You'd have to return to Hatfield to do that."

"He wouldn't dare leave it at home where his mama might see it. He brought it to London with him. Since he hasn't been to his flat yet, it must be in his carriage."

"He and Breslau are using Breslau's carriage."

A sly gleam lit Nigel's pale eyes. "Maxwell would have his driver stable his rig, but he'd drop the luggage off at his flat first. I believe we shall pay a call on old Maxwell, Pam."

"We'd learn more if we followed Breslau and Max."

"We can easily pick up their trail. They'll be at the theater for hours. Wes virtually lives there, and there's nothing Maxwell likes better than ogling the actresses. What bothers me is how I am to get into Maxwell's bedroom to search for the bracelet."

Pamela knew him well enough to realize she would save more time in the long run by going along with him. "I could rip my gown, and ask for a needle and thread. If his flat is small, they'll have to let me use his bedchamber to fix the rent. You keep the servants occupied, and I'll search."

"That's a capital idea! He lives on the way to Drury Lane, too, so we shan't waste much time if he's hidden the bracelet somewhere else."

What did waste considerable time was deciding what transportation could be used. The general's carriage had left. Nigel was leery of taking Wes's curricle and bays. What he actually feared was that the groom wouldn't let him have them, and he didn't want the humiliation of being refused in front of Pamela. In the end, they went into the street and hired a cab.

From that point on, things went remarkably smoothly. Nigel had acting blood in his veins. He made a believable story of wanting to see the general, and of Miss Comstock having ripped her sleeve when she reached to a high shelf to select a bolt of worsted at a drapery shop. Before you could say Jack Robinson, she was alone in the general's bedchamber, wasting her time by looking for a diamond bracelet which she knew perfectly well was not there. Her job was made easier by the presence of Maxwell's unpacked luggage on the floor at the end of his bed.

She unfastened it and rifled quickly through the stacks of linen and stockings. There was no diamond bracelet, but she did find a ring in a small leather box. It was a rather fine sapphire, set all around in small diamonds. She didn't remove the ring, but as soon as they left, she described it to Nigel.

"Max brought that home from India with him eons ago. His mama and his sisters are forever trying to get it from him, but he's keeping it for his own wife, if he can ever find anyone indiscriminating enough to have him."

"Since he brought it to London at this time he must plan to propose to Fleur. He can't know she's dead, Nigel. You must be mistaken about that."

"Who's to say he hadn't given it to her before, and went to get it back from her at Belmont the night before last? It pretty well proves his guilt in my opinion."

"There's no point trying to convince you with facts. Your mind is made up."

This was the side of Pamela he found least lovable. He remembered what a shrew she could be, and turned sulky. "What do you want to do then?"

"Go to Drury Lane."

"We'd be better off checking out Newman's Stables to see if the rig Halton hired is back yet." As this was of some interest, Pamela agreed to go there first.

"What's so important about that particular rig?" the stableman asked suspiciously. "Has it got something to do with Fleur's murder? I already have orders from Lord Breslau to send word the minute it lands in, and let him know who was driving it. If you want a lad to notify you as well, it'll cost you a crown."

"Never mind," Nigel said.

"Now may we go to Drury Lane?" Pamela asked, in exactly the tone of voice he liked least.

"Damme Fleur ain't at Drury Lane. You heard the man say the rig ain't back yet. I have half a mind to go to Belmont."

"Then you will please drop me off at Drury Lane."

"Yes, to roll your eyes at Breslau. Don't think I don't know what's going on. I see you've been cranking your hair into ringlets. You'll catch cold if you think to make any headway in that direction, my girl."

A surge of suppressed anger rose up and engulfed Pamela. "You impertinent puppy!" It was the charge of chasing Breslau that hit home, but she had more ammunition to wound him in a different direction.

"I've wasted quite enough time pandering to your stupidity. Any fool can see General Maxwell is in love with Fleur and worried sick at her disappearance. Bear in mind it was your own father's coat and galoshes that were covered in mud, *your* badger sett where her shawl was found, *your* father who gave her the diamond bracelet, and *your* house from which she disappeared. I hope for your sake Fleur is alive, for if she's dead, it's not General Maxwell who will dance on the end of a rope."

Bereft of a sensible reply, Nigel said, "You sound for the world like Mama when you go into one of your rants. You might as well blame me as Papa."

"Don't think it hasn't occurred to me. You only blame Maxwell because you're jealous of him. Jealousy has led to murder before now. You were loathe to share the profits of your drama with Fleur, too. With her dead, you could keep all the money yourself."

"If we're talking about jealousy, don't leave your old favorite out. Breslau's in love with her, too, you know, which don't prevent him from using her death for cheap publicity. And why is he so eager to know when the carriage gets back to Newman's Stables? He wants to get hold of the driver and make sure he don't talk. He probably plans to murder *him*, too. Papa saw him skulking around the corridor by her apartment the night she disappeared. What was Breslau doing there at one o'clock in the morning?"

"What was your father doing there?" she countered.

"Trying to get back the bracelet she bought."

They glared at each other, then Pamela said, "If you're returning to Belmont, pray leave me off at Drury Lane."

"That I'll not."

"Then I shall walk," she said, and turned to do just that.

Nigel sulkily agreed to deliver her. As the carriage progressed toward its destination, he began talking himself out of returning to Belmont.

"I think you should go," Pamela told him. "It's your neighborhood. You would know better than anyone else where Fleur might be. Are there any empty houses in the neighborhood?"

"No," he answered, without even considering the matter.

A little later he continued. "If Fleur were alive, which she ain't, don't think she'd let Max hide her in some cold and lonely, old abandoned house. The place she'd hide is right here in London, where she could hear all the gossip about her disappearance."

"Yes, if her kidnapper was that considerate," she said ironically. "And in that case, the carriage would be back at Newman's. You're speaking as though she had kidnapped herself." Pamela stopped and thought about what she had said. "Could she possibly be so conniving?"

After a judicious pause for mind-changing, Nigel allowed that she might. "The sliest woman in London. It was very cagey the way she got me to ask her to Belmont, now I think of it. And she only did it to be near Maxwell."

"How did she convince you? I was amazed you ever asked her, Nigel, knowing how your mother would feel."

"I dropped around her flat one afternoon—to work on the memoirs, you know. We were always interrupted a dozen times, but that day there wasn't a minute's peace. Her modiste came, and her hairdresser."

"They wouldn't come without an appointment."

"She put them up to it, certainly. Two or three runners came from Drury Lane. Spiedel dropped in."

"I wager he was invited, too."

"And half a dozen other hangers on. She said how impossible it was to work there, and would it not be better if we went away somewhere. Truth to tell, I thought she meant just the two of us—I hardly knew which way to look. But it soon came out it was Belmont she meant. She was so enthusiastic about it, you know, and I could hardly tell her Mama would have me minced and fed to the carrion crows. I told her Belmont would be pretty well filled up, but she kept at me till I had to ask her, so I did, and got Wes to come along. He can handle her. But *she* put me up to it."

Nigel fell into a fit of silent concentration. When he revived, he had completely switched his opinion of Fleur around. "And she asked the deuce of a lot of questions about Papa, too," he said accusingly. "Letting on she was only interested in me. How much money would Papa leave me, and a dozen questions about his youth. Brighton, in particular. I say, Pam, you don't suppose there was anything between them?"

"Possibly. Your father was handsome when he was young."

"You wouldn't know about it, for you're not the type, but to tell the truth, he still has a streak of tomcat in him."

"I do know it."

"Pam, you don't mean he's been trying to get *you* into corners!"

"No! No, but I am aware of his—his reputation," she said, softening the charge with a forgiving smile.

"Imagine Fleur dunning Papa. I should like to have witnessed that scene. He'd kill her." Nigel's eyes flew open at what had slipped out. "Only speaking metaphorically!"

"Of course. He wouldn't have given her the bracelet if he meant to—to silence her more permanently. Let us not waste time discussing anything so ridiculous."

Nigel had turned quite pale. "Perhaps Papa was

165

in her apartment the night she disappeared, to try to get the bracelet back. He might have given it to her to keep her quiet till he had an opportunity to—silence her more permanently," he said, borrowing Pamela's phrase. The word *murder* stuck in his throat. "There's no denying he has a wretched temper."

"Breslau didn't seem at all worried, Nigel. I am convinced he knows something. What he doesn't know is where Fleur is hiding. That is what we must discover. Now think where she would go if she wanted to disappear for a few days."

"She was pretty close with Spiedel."

"We've been there, and to Henry Halton's place as well. Is there someone else?"

"She has a bunch of French friends scattered around the city. And she knows actresses all over the country, from her days in the provinces. She calls actors her real family. I wouldn't have a notion where to begin looking."

They discussed possibilities till the carriage reached Drury Lane. The front door was locked, and Nigel had the pleasure of showing off his familiarity with the place by going to the rear door. At noon, the theater was practically deserted. A stagehand told them Breslau and General Maxwell had been there talking to Rose Flanders, but left an hour ago.

"The Drury Lane Restaurant!" Pamela exclaimed.

The place was in an uproar discussing Fleur's disappearance. It took several minutes to scan the crowd and assure themselves Breslau and Max were not there. After a few questions, they learned they hadn't been there. No one had seen them since they left the theater.

"Breslau's out setting Rose up in a love nest," one wag suggested.

"Aye, Fleur's death was the making of Rose Flanders. She'll be his new leading lady, both on the stage and off."

"Is that the reputation Breslau enjoys?" Pamela asked when they returned to the carriage.

"He wouldn't waste his time on Rose. He has much prettier flirts than that. It's just business, getting her signed to replace Fleur at a bargain price. Mind you, that ain't to say he hadn't got eyes for Fleur. She was different. More cunning," he added grimly.

The idea was taking root in his head that the play might show Fleur in a less attractive light than the memoirs. A bit of a vixen, toying with young gentlemen, scattering broken hearts to left and right. He became aware that the gnawing at his vitals was not all due to Fleur's perfidy.

"It's time for fork work," he said. "Do you want to return to Breslau House, or eat in peace at a restaurant?"

Breslau House without Breslau held no charm, and she opted for a restaurant. Over lunch, they continued discussing the case.

"Let us go back to Spiedel's and Halton's flats," Pam suggested. "They are the only solid leads we have."

They went first to Spiedel's, with no real hope of discovering anything. As they drew near the corner of Drury Lane and Macklin Street, Pamela scanned doorways, trying to recognize Spiedel's building.

"There, that's it. The one with the carriage out front. Nigel, you don't think it could be Fleur! It's a traveling carriage."

Nigel's face had turned to ash. "It's Papa's carriage!" he whispered.

# Chapter Eleven

Nigel's surprise was hardly greater than Miss Comstock's. "What could Sir Aubrey be doing here?" she asked.

He pulled the check string but made no move to leave the carriage. "I can't face him, Pam."

"We'll wait till he leaves, and ask Mr. Spiedel what he wanted."

It was five minutes before a hag-ridden Sir Aubrey came out. He looked up and down the street nervously, apparently finding nothing suspicious in a lingering cab. He hopped into his carriage and drove away at a smart clip.

As soon as he rounded the corner, Pamela and Nigel alit and hastened to Mr. Spiedel's doorway. They were admitted by his factotum and shown into Mr. Spiedel's modest living room. Thus far, Mr. Spiedel was only a name to Pamela. She had formed a mental picture of what he would be like—something of a dandy, handsome in a second class sort of way. She was not prepared for a regular Adonis, but that was what she found herself gazing at. If he was Fleur's *cher ami*, she had to approve the actress's taste.

Mr. Spiedel was no stripling like Nigel. Though young, he was well-formed, with a man's broad shoulders and full chest. His clothing was genteel without being flashy. Hair the shade of a ripe chestnut, and as glossy, sat on his well-shaped head. His regular features were lent charm by the intelligence in his brown eyes. His manners, too, were more than acceptable.

"Mr. Raleigh, isn't it?" he said, shaking Nigel's hand. "I believe we met at Lady Chamaude's place." He turned a questioning face toward Pamela, and Nigel introduced them.

"I've never had so much company in my life," Mr. Spiedel said, and laughed. "Your father just left, and before him, Lord Alban came to call. I never met either of them before in my life."

"What did Papa want?" Nigel asked.

"Like Lord Alban, he came to offer his assistance—Fleur has been speaking to them, I assume. She has promised in the past to help me land a position. Thus far I haven't had the offer I really want. I wish to become an actor. Convent Garden has offered me a speaking part, hardly enough to live on. I haven't accepted it, though I was just reading in the morning papers that I have. Alban wanted me to act as his secretary, and Sir Aubrey has offered—er, financial assistance in whatever project I choose to undertake. Very generous of him."

"How much?" Nigel asked jealously.

Mr. Spiedel smiled. "Not enough for you to worry about, Mr. Raleigh. Your father hardly plans to beggar his family for a virtual stranger. I am amazed that he came at all. Is he some kin to Lady Chamaude?"

"Certainly not!"

Mr. Spiedel's laughing eyes skimmed in Pamela's direction, but he said nothing. The feeling was in the air all the same that there was something between Fleur and Nigel's father. Pamela studied Mr. Spiedel for any resemblance to Sir Aubrey, and found none. This fine-featured face was not in the Raleigh style. That left Lord Alban as Spiedel's natural father. Surely that was the connection between this disparate group.

"Did Sir Aubrey mention Lady Chamaude?" Pamela asked.

The handsome eyes clouded over with apprehension. "He knew her some years ago and, of course, she was visiting him recently. He has no idea where she is now. He asked me in particular if I had heard from her since she left Belmont. Those articles in the morning papers have put the fear of God into me."

"Where's he putting up?" Nigel demanded.

"At the Reddleston."

"I take it you've been looking for the marquise?" Pamela asked.

"I've called on every person I ever heard her mention. No one has seen her. I can't believe she's dead. Who would kill such a charming, harmless lady? Fleur hasn't an enemy in the world. I refuse to consider the other possibility."

"What do you mean, Mr. Spiedel?" Pamela asked. His frown deepened. "I'm talking about suicide."

"Oh, no! She'd never do that!"

Spiedel shook his head doubtfully. "In the normal way she wouldn't, but when I read of General Maxwell's visiting Lady Margaret Irving, I wondered—"

"But he isn't!" she exclaimed.

"I read it in the *Morning Post*. Lady Margaret had nearly brought the general up to scratch before he met Fleur, you must know. I feared his mother must have ordered him to marry Lady Margaret when he was at home visiting her."

"It wouldn't surprise me in the least," Nigel scowled. "It was even in the papers."

Pamela considered this problem a moment, then said, "It seems the papers have published more than one piece of false information today, does it not? Your having accepted the offer from Convent Garden, Mr. Spiedel, and Maxwell's visiting Lady Margaret. That is rather—odd," she said. Nigel paid no heed to the meaningful look she bestowed on him. His eyes were fully occupied in studying Spiedel's cravat, which had a fine, careless air, yet was decidedly stylish.

Pamela felt in her bones that Lord Breslau was involved in all these misleading announcements. Why else had he been smiling over the papers at breakfast? Of more importance, why had he sent them in? She was fairly sure by this time that Breslau was also responsible for announcing Fleur's disappearance. That, at least, was true. And where did Lord Alban fit into any of it?

"When Lord Alban called, did he mention Fleur?" she asked Spiedel.

"Not by name. He said a friend had recommended me very highly. I know Fleur is acquainted with his lordship. More than acquainted; the friendship goes back several years. Certainly it was Fleur who brought me to his attention."

"Have any other gentlemen called offering favors?"

172

His smile was disarmingly frank. "Not so far, but the day is young. Ah, there is the door knocker now!"

While his guests looked at each other in consternation, a Mr. Webb was shown in. He, too, was a prosperous-looking gentleman of middle years, a strange to Mr. Spiedel, but presumably not to Fleur. He wished for a moment's privacy with Mr. Spiedel to discuss a business matter.

Nigel and Pamela left. As they returned to the carriage, they were too confused for rational conversation. Ideas darted around in their heads, looking for a pattern. The announcement of Fleur's death had brought a host of middle-aged, well-to-do gentlemen calling on Mr. Spiedel offering assistance. The reason was staring them in the face. They felt they owed Spiedel something, that the young man had some claim on them. The only possible idea Pam could come up with was that one of them was Spiedel's father, and Fleur his mother. Mr. Spiedel couldn't be aware of it. He was genuinely bewildered at all the offers showered on him.

The marquise's apparently casual remarks at Belmont assumed a new significance. Pamela scoured her mind to recall what she had said. "You'd be surprised what talking over the old days can bring up. Alban, for instance, has been most helpful. All my old friends are very generous in assisting me." Surely they hadn't *all* saddled her with pledges of their troth? Spiedel was the only young man they were rushing to assist, unless Henry Halton, too, had been receiving offers. He couldn't though. He wasn't to be found.

Of course, the clever marquise could be telling each of her erstwhile lovers that he was the father.

The words *your son* had definitely been overheard at Belmont. Blackmail hardly seemed too strong a word for her stunt. Had one of her victims decided to kill Fleur rather than pay up? Breslau wouldn't be filling the papers with lies if Fleur were dead. What would be the point? Indeed she could see no point in it whether Fleur was dead or alive.

If she were dead she'd never read them, and if she were alive it would only infuriate her. Every item was an offense: that General Maxwell had deserted her, that her son was joining the theater when her aim was to keep him out of it, that Rose Flanders was to replace her in the new play. Breslau would be fortunate if Fleur didn't come dashing back and murder him. A flash of understanding struck her and she gasped. So that was it!

"We might as well take a run over to Halton's place," Nigel said.

"It isn't necessary. We can go home now."

"I'm going to the Reddleston and have it out with Papa. What business has he giving my patrimony to Mr. Spiedel? If he thinks Mama will stand still for that, he has another think coming."

Should she tell him? No, that was Sir Aubrey's secret, to share if he wished. One of the marquise's victims must actually be Spiedel's father. One of them owed him and Fleur something. And if it was unsure which one was the father, then each should pay a part. Fleur wasn't asking so much, to judge by Spiedel's words. "Not enough to beggar him." It would teach them all a lesson.

While Nigel rambled on, Pamela sat thinking. She decided that she couldn't despise the ingenious marquise. All her scheming was not for herself. She just

wanted a little security for her son. She wanted him
to be respectable, to take a job in the government
rather than be an actor like herself. Who knew better than Fleur what hardships the acting life entailed? Always an outsider, hanging on the fringes
of society, acceptable enough to the gentlemen for an
evening's entertainment, but not good enough to be
presented to their families. It must be a lonesome
sort of life. No wonder if actresses took lovers. It
seemed they couldn't have husbands, unless they
were as fortunate as Mrs. Siddons and married a famous actor.

What she could not figure out was the strange
manner of Fleur's disappearance. Why had she been
playing dead when Nigel went to her room? Why did
first the marquise vanish, then her clothes? And
most of all, where was she? The answer, she thought,
would be revealed at the theater that evening. When
Nigel stopped at the Reddleston Hotel, Pamela had
the carriage deliver her to Breslau House.

Lord Breslau had been home and left again. Miss
Agatha handed her a note and a newspaper. "Breslau left these for you. He thought you might be interested in the entertainment pages, Miss
Comstock," she said. All smiles had dissipated. Miss
Agatha looked as if she'd just had all her teeth
drawn. "And by the by, Mrs. Foster came to call
while you were out. I had to tell her I had no idea
where you were, or when you would be home. She
was extremely upset. I suggest you go to her, or at
least write her a note explaining what you are doing
here."

The malicious glint hinted that Miss Agatha would
not mind an explanation herself. There was no longer

any need for conciliation. Mrs. Foster had used the words "Miss Comstock's intended" in connection with Mr. Raleigh.

"Thank you," Pamela said, and darted upstairs with her note and the paper.

Breslau had the paper folded back to the appropriate page. Several items were circled in red ink. She read them even before opening her note. The longest was an article praising Rose Flanders to the sky in her interpretation of Emily in *The Deuce Is in Him.* The words "she came, she was seen, she conquered," "not since Mrs. Siddons," and other unlikely hyperboles jumped out at her. They smacked of Breslau's mannered speech. If this didn't bring Fleur back, then they would have to assume she was dead.

The first item was obviously calculated to throw Fleur into a pelter. It was the second that brought Pamela to her feet with a shriek of outrage.

Theater lovers will be crowding the greenroom of Drury Lane this evening. The rumor is abroad that Lord B—— will be hosting a party and making a surprise announcement. Dare we hope the surprise is his new play, and new leading lady?

After reading the gushing review of Rose Flanders, one would have be to dull not to guess who this "lady" might be. What infuriated Pamela was the location of the party, the greenroom.

It was impossible for a real lady to visit the greenroom. Breslau had chosen the spot on purpose to exclude her from the excitement. He could have had it—well, not at Breslau House perhaps, but at an ho-

176

tel, where it would only be shabby for her to attend, and not impossible. The announcement put Breslau's note completely out of her mind, but when she threw the paper across the room in a fit of temper, the note fell to the ground and she snatched it up.

Even the unexpectedly warm salutation didn't lessen her wrath. "Dearest Pam," she read with a derisive snort.

Read the underlined items in the papers before reading this. Sorry about the greenroom, but with all my starched relations, I must keep my work and my private life separate. I have a strong intuition this bash will be awash in infamy and bad histrionics. Even a restaurant is too public. Do come to the theater, though. Tickets enclosed for a private box. Perhaps the Fosters would like to accompany you? If you can stay awake till one or two, I shall tell all when I return. Please don't remove to the Fosters' to repay me for my recent annoying stunts. I must see you tonight. It is urgent. I believe we have discussed before the inconvenient urgency pertaining to certain relationships? Best love, Breslau.

Pamela's frown faded momentarily and a bemused smile hovered over her features. This was his way of telling her the meeting tonight was a love tryst. How strange that Breslau should have succumbed to her when she hadn't even tried to attract him. He was much too high for her. Yet despite his aristocratic looks and his habitual air of ennui, Breslau—Wes— had an unexpectedly jolly and common streak in him. He loved the brawling theater life and theater people. A toplofty lord would have no use for such things.

She admitted to strong emotional stirrings when he tried to kiss her. Her heart had pounded furiously. Even before that—last night at the theater when she felt his eyes resting on her—she had been aware of a growing interest in him. It had seemed too foolish to let the feeling have its head. For some time she sat, her mind roaming over new and happy ideas.

But as she reread the items underscored in the papers, her frown returned. It seemed Breslau intended to keep all the fun to himself. *He* might go to the greenroom and enjoy the infamy and bad histrionics while *she* was to sit in the box, out of it all. In a pig's eye she would! If there was ever to be anything between them, he must realize she meant to share his whole life. She would attend the party at the greenroom, which meant not inviting the Fosters, and that was a great pity. They would have enjoyed the play.

Of course, she couldn't attend alone. She flipped the tickets, pondering who to ask. Nigel was the obvious choice, but would he take her? What if Sir Aubrey tagged along? Very likely Nigel was still with him at the Reddleston. If not, she must discover exactly where Nigel's apartment was located and visit him there. He had a flat somewhere on Soho Square.

Further problems came to bedevil her. A glance in her mirror told her she would be as out of place in a greenroom as Hanna More at an orgy. A disguise then. Oh, dear, and that meant going to Bond Street to hire a wig and outfit. She drew a deep sigh. Calling on the Fosters made an unexceptionable excuse to have a cab called. She would tell Miss Agatha she was going to her aunt's. As she really had to tell the Fosters something, she scribbled up a hasty note saying she was busy that evening, but would call tomorrow, and bribed a footman to deliver it.

As soon as this was done, she put on her pelisse and bonnet and went belowstairs.

"Not taking your luggage with you, Miss Comstock?" Miss Agatha enquired.

"No, Lord Breslau most particularly asked me to remain another night." She smiled demurely.

"Hmph. Will you be home to dinner?"

"Certainly I shall. Lord Breslau will not be here, however."

"He didn't say so!"

"He told me, Miss Agatha. I shall be going out this evening. Don't wait up for us."

"Us?"

"Did I not mention it? I shall be joining Wes. We'll be rather late."

Miss Agatha looked as if she'd just been bitten by a snake. Wes, was it? An angry retort transformed itself to a confused smile. "Very well, Miss Comstock. I shall tell Cook. Dinner for three. Or will your intended, Mr. Raleigh, be joining us?" she asked, and looked sharp for the answer.

"I'm not engaged, Miss Agatha. Where did you get such an idea?"

Miss Agatha just stared. "Will Mr. Raleigh be joining us?"

"No, he shan't. There will be just the three of us."

On this phrase Pamela swept out to wait for the cab. She gave directions to the Reddleston Hotel and

179

had the cab wait while she went in to enquire for Mr. Raleigh.

"Sir Aubrey, do you mean? He has gone out."

"No, his son, Mr. Nigel Raleigh. Is he in?"

"He was in the taproom with his father. I didn't see him leave. I'll have a look."

Within minutes, Nigel was in the cab with Pamela, absolutely prohibiting her plans for the night. "What would Mama say, you dressing up in my breeches and jacket and going to a greenroom?"

"I trust you won't tell her. I mean to go, with or without your assistance, Nigel. It's going to be a very interesting party. Would you not like to come?"

"I have to work. Since Papa is giving away a thousand pounds to a total stranger, it seems I will have to support myself."

"A thousand pounds, eh? Did he say why?"

Nigel gave a disgruntled snort. "It seems Spiedel is the orphan son of a friend of his. A bunch of the old crones are getting together and taking up a subscription for the lad. His father died recently, and had run through his estate. Very generous of Papa, I'm sure, handing a thousand pounds over to a stranger. Oh, and incidentally, Pam, he don't want you to mention it to Mama."

"Of course. It has nothing to do with me."

"And about Mama's diamond bracelet—"

"Yes?" she asked eagerly.

"It was Fleur who started up this whole collection for Spiedel. She knew his mama, you see. She'd been giving Spiedel a little money herself from time to time to keep him out of the poorhouse, since the fellow refuses to ever do an honest day's work. I told you how generous she is, but naturally she can't assume his whole upkeep herself. She spoke to some of the late Mr. Spiedel's friends and started the ball rolling. Papa was short of blunt, so he donated the bracelet since Mama never wears it. But then he thought better of it, and decided he could spare the money if he put off getting the stalls fixed. That's why he was visiting Fleur's room the night she disappeared, but she was already gone. I daresay the bracelet will turn up when they find Fleur's body, and we'll get it back. You'd best not mention the bracelet to Mama, either."

"There is no reason why I should."

So that was to be the story. Very well. It cast a lovely, generous glow over all the miscreants, and kept Mr. Spiedel in the dark about his true parentage. She wondered if Fleur herself knew which one was the boy's father.

"About tonight, Nigel . . ."

"I've already told you, I ain't going."

"As you are editing Fleur's memoirs, and dramatizing them for the stage, should you not be there?"

"What has this got to do with Fleur? It is to be Rose Flander's party."

"But only think if Fleur isn't dead at all. If she's only been—captured by French spies," she said, grasping wildly for something to appeal to his romanticism. "The papers mentioned the possibility. She might escape and come to the greenroom. You wouldn't want to miss that."

"By Jove, Pam! What a bunch of dunderheads we are! We haven't even *begun* to look into that possibility! She is often pestered by the Frenchies trying to get her to work for them."

"She is so very clever, she might very well escape."

"I shouldn't put it a pace past her."

"So you'll lend me a jacket and a pair of trousers. You are so sma— so lean and elegant. I could wear your clothing without much adjustment. Why don't we go around to your apartment now and get them?"

"There's no need for you to put yourself to so much trouble, Pam. You would hate rubbing elbows with cits and rakes."

At her wits' end, Pamela put her hand trustingly in his. "I want to be with you, Nigel." She smiled. "I cannot go without a disguise."

Nigel looked first shocked, then gratified. "I never knew you was such a game chick, Pam. If you're up to it, then I'll help you, but for God's sake don't let Breslau see you. Hang in the shadows. Not that he'll be paying any heed to you now that he's decided to make Rose his new flirt."

"Thank you, Nigel." She smiled. "There is just one more thing. I shall need a place to change. I'll wear my gown when I leave Breslau House, and change at your apartment."

"You can't come to a bachelor's apartment."

"I can't change in the carriage. You can scout out the building, and I'll go in when no one is around."

"I suppose that would be all right. At least Papa hasn't taken into his noggin to attend the play. He's going to a concert of antique music. I near choked when he told me. He's been talking like Mama this trip. All about the evil of the theater. He tried to forbid me to write the play for Fleur, but when I pointed out there was a thousand pounds to be made up from his giving Spiedel our money, he tucked in his horns pretty quick."

"You *are* clever." She smiled approvingly.

"It seems everyone knows it but me. Here is Breslau begging me to write a play for Drury Lane. Always was a bit of a modest fellow," he boasted.

"I've often noticed it. You didn't pull the check string, Nigel. We're going to your flat now."

"No need, since you're going to change there tonight."

"That's true," she said, blinking in surprise that he should have thought of it.

"Just leave everything to me, m'dear. I say, Pam, don't you think it's time we discussed setting the date for our wedding? Best to get on with it."

Pamela felt like screaming. She gave a grimace that was halfway between a smile and frown. "Later."

"You can leave that up to me as well. I rather think St. George's in Hanover for the ceremony. You don't mind if we're married in London? As a dramatist, I'll have to make my home here. You'll want a few weeks treacle moon in the city before you go back to Belmont and start filling our nursery."

In a thin voice, Pamela said, "I'll just leave all that up to you, Nigel."

He smiled contentedly and drew her arm through his. Before it had quite come to rest, Pamela found an excuse to remove it. Such was Nigel's passion that he didn't bother to pursue her errant fingers.

## Chapter Twelve

It was eight o'clock when Mr. Patrick Ryder stood in front of Nigel's mirror in borrowed breeches and trousers to examine herself for telltale signs of femininity. Patrick Ryder was the name chosen for Pamela, in case anyone should enquire. The clothing fit disconcertingly well. With her hair tied back and the linen stock nestling against her chin, Pamela felt she could pass for a very young gentleman, one who was not yet put to the inconvenience of a regular shave. The wadding in the borrowed jacket lent her an impressive set of shoulders. With the jacket closed, she managed to conceal the hasty stitches that kept the breeches from slipping down. Nigel was quick to point out that he had had that outfit since university. It no longer fit him, but was too good to throw out.

"There won't be a gentleman under thirty wearing silk stockings and knee breeches," he worried. "All the bucks have switched to pantaloons. I shall have to say you're a country cousin. That might account for it, and for the antique hairdo as well. You look a quiz, Pam."

"I think I look very handsome," she decided, turning this way and that. "I need some wadding for the toes of these slippers, though. They shuffle when I walk. Can you lend me some handkerchiefs?"

The handkerchiefs were brought forth, two in each slipper, and with them in place, Pamela practiced walking back and forth with her toes slightly turned out, to give her a more masculine strut.

"Just stick to the shadows, and you'll do," Nigel decided. "No one will take a second look during the show. We'll keep our seat after the performance till the greenroom has had a chance to fill up. Let me do the talking. Your voice is a dead giveaway."

Pamela tightened her throat and spoke in a gruff voice. "Oh, I say, Nigel old boy, a chap can't stand silent as a jug all night, what?"

He stared in amusement. "How did you do that?"

"I copied Papa."

"Don't do it again."

"Why not?"

He frowned in distaste. "You do it too well. You don't even seem like a girl."

"That's the whole point, ain't it?"

"Now you're using men's words. I wish you would stop it, Pam."

"Jolly good sport. What say we stop at a tavern for a wet before the play, eh?"

"We're late already," he scowled, and stalked out of the apartment without holding the door for her.

No one gave Pamela a second look when they alit to enter the theater. A few heads turned after they were seated, but heads always turned to see who was occupying Lord Breslau's box. The occupants that evening were not of sufficient interest to keep many glasses trained on them. They didn't even see the one pair of glasses that studied them for several minutes. Their holder stood at the edge of the stage, concealed behind the curtain. Lord Breslau was not greatly surprised. He had rather expected Pam would come masqueraded in a blond wig, but so long as she was there, he was content.

When he had confirmed that the young gentleman with Nigel was Pamela, he looked once more to the pit. It was a lady all dressed in black that intrigued him. What had first drawn his attention to her was the heavy veil covering her face. He had never seen the bonnet before, but it was stylish dramatic. The next few hours were only a time to be endured by all till the real excitement began.

Nigel had seen the play dozens of times, and Pamela had seen it just the night before. Nigel passed the time by scanning the boxes and pit for his father. Secure that Sir Aubrey had not come, he said at the first intermission that he was going for a stroll and would be back presently.

"I'm going with you," Pamela said at once, and rose.

"No, you ain't. I don't plan to be seen on the strut with a flat wearing a monkey suit."

She acquiesced with a celerity that a brighter man would have found suspicious. As soon as Nigel was gone, Pam left the box and went alone into the hallway, where theatergoers stood in clusters, laughing, flirting, and occasionally talking about the performance. Idle curiosity to see how the great disported themselves when at leisure was not her only motive. Naturally she would keep her eyes and ears open for anything that might relate to Fleur's disappearance. A glimpse of Mr. Spiedel would have been welcome. Catching Breslau out in a flirtation even moreso.

What she did not expect to see was the mysterious stranger from the assembly at Hatfield. When she spotted him along the corridor, she thought she was imagining things. A second look assured her it was definitely the man presumed to be Mr. Henry Halton. He was alone, and he was carrying his coat over his arm, which suggested that he had just arrived. Before long, she decided he was behaving suspiciously. Not that he exactly did anything other than nod and speak to a few people, but he had a wary way of looking over his shoulder, of scanning the crowd as though—well, as though guilty of murder.

Her next thought was to notify Breslau. As he had not bothered to visit her in his box during intermission, this meant finding her way backstage. Unfortunately, going backstage would cause her to lose sight of Mr. Halton. She stood, undecided, looking around for Nigel. Where was the pest of a boy when she needed him? As she stood uncertainly, Mr. Halton turned on his heel and left the corridor. He didn't head toward any of the boxes, but to the staircase that would take him out of the theater. Panic seized her. He was getting away, and she was helpless to prevent him. The bell clanged, calling the theatergoers back to their seats. Crowds thronged around her, and when she looked toward the staircase again, Mr. Halton was gone.

Without another thought, she ran down the stairs after him. The door was just closing. She waited a moment before opening it and going out into the cold night. The winter wind tore through her light jacket and whistled up her spine. Lucky Mr. Halton was putting his coat on before striking out into the street. He turned and glanced at her. She looked off into the distance, hoping to give the idea she was awaiting a carriage.

Mr. Halton turned again and said, "Would you happen to have a light?" She saw he held a cheroot in his fingers.

She consciously lowered her voice. "Afraid not."

Halton nodded and turned away. She went after him and fell into step. "A chilly night, eh?" she said conversationally.

"Dammed cold. There's never a cab when you want one."

"I'm looking for one myself. Perhaps we could share. Ryder's the name."

Mr. Halton appeared not uninterested. "Which way are you going, Mr. Ryder?"

"I don't mind—just out of the cold. Where are you off to then, Mr.—?"

"Halton," he said briefly. "I don't know. Perhaps I'll just go home."

It wasn't necessary to ask where home was. It immediately occurred to her that if he was going to Wild Street, he would hardly require a cab it was so close. She continued walking with him. In a moment Mr. Halton said, "There's a cab coming now. I shan't be joining you. Good night."

He gave a salute and continued on at a faster pace. Pamela hailed the cab, but instead of hiring it, she just asked the driver where Convent Gardens was. When she saw Mr. Halton turn into Wild Street, she thanked the driver and hurried after Halton. Wild

Street proved to be a veritable slum. The only light was the dim reflection from a few windows shining on the broken cobblestone underfoot. Curiosity urged her to follow her quarry, but caution pulled her back toward the relative safety of Drury Lane.

Mr. Halton was no longer visible in the dark tunnellike laneway. Suspicious noises issued from the alleys between houses, sounding at times like a menacing whisper, at others like the rustle of scurrying cats or rodents. Her brow moistened in fear, and her heart thumped like a motor. At the entrance to the second alley, Pamela's courage deserted her. She stopped and turned to leave. Before she had retreated two steps, there was a sudden movement of air behind her. A heavy hand fell on her shoulder and Mr. Halton said, "Are you following me, Mr. Ryder?" in an extremely menacing voice.

Now where the deuce had Pam got herself off to? Nigel glanced occasionally toward the rear of the box as the second act began. The flat likely didn't know the bell meant it was time to return to your box. Where did she think all the patrons were going? He wasn't in the least surprised that she had left, but when ten minutes passed and still she didn't return, he began to worry. Might be best just to slip around backstage and see if she was pestering Wes. No where else she could be, really.

He ran Breslau to ground in his office on the second story at the rear of the building. Every elegance and convenience had been added to the spacious chamber at his lordship's own expense. Breslau didn't like to be disturbed here, but on this occasion he peered over Nigel's shoulder with more pleasure than chagrin. When he saw that Nigel was alone, his smile faded.

"I hope you haven't abandoned Miss Comstock in the box," he said.

"She ain't in the box, Wes. That's why I'm here. She left. I was sure she would be with you."

A frown seized Breslau's austere features. "What do you mean, she isn't in the box? She was there during the first act."

"How'd you know that?"

"Never mind. When did she leave, and why didn't you go with her?"

"I told her to stay there when I left at the intermission. She must have slipped out while my back was turned."

Breslau was on his feet, hastening toward the greenroom. Even while the play was in progress, this famous meeting spot was busy. A quick glance around showed him she wasn't there. A dash to various dressing rooms and a few barked questions told him she hadn't been seen in any of the likely places.

"What happened? Did she see someone in the audience . . . Fleur or Halton or Spiedel?"

Nigel shook his head. "She didn't say so if she did. Well she couldn't have, for I scoured the place very thoroughly looking for Papa, and didn't spot any of them."

"It must have happened during intermission. She saw Halton or Spiedel and the greenhead decided to follow him."

Breslau was aware of a gnawing anxiety that threatened to cause nausea. Awful visions reared up in his mind of Pamela at the mercy of some street ruffian. It didn't even occur to him that she was destroying his well-orchestrated evening's entertainment. His face paled and his eyes stared into the distance, while a fierce frown of concentration pulled his brows together.

"Are you all right?" Nigel asked.

"If anything's happened to her, I'll see you in Newgate," he replied, and strode rapidly for the closest exit, with Nigel in hot pursuit.

"Nothing's happened to her. She's dressed like a man, if you're worried some fop has attacked her. None of your business in any case. I can look after my own fiancée."

"She's not marrying you, you cretin," he said grimly over his shoulder.

"Is she not? It might interest you to know we've set the date and chosen St. George's for the wedding."

"Excellent. All we have to do is change the bridegroom."

Breslau made curt enquiries of the minions of Drury Lane. One of them had noticed the young gentleman in breeches and silk stockings dart out without a coat just as the second-act bell was ringing. He wondered that the gentleman hadn't returned. Outside, there were two grooms in charge of traffic. Both of them had noticed two young gents having a word. They'd strolled off together, one of them without a jacket, too. He'd take his death. No, they hadn't got into a carriage.

Breslau, also without a jacket, flew down Russell Street, around the corner to Drury Lane, trying to think. He had spoken to Spiedel before the play and could conceive of no reason why he should harm Pamela. The unknown quantity was Mr. Hal-

191

ton. His steps turned toward Wild Street. Of course it would be the most depraved street in London that the hoyden chose for her investigation. Obviously Halton had decided to visit the theater. He should have warned Nigel to keep a closer eye on the girl. Better, he should have stayed with her himself.

"I'll tell you flat, Pam ain't here," Nigel decided when the shadows grew impenetrable and rustling sounds from the alleys convinced him no one but a lunatic would venture unprotected into such an area.

"Go back to the theater if you're afraid."

"I ain't, but Pam would be. She ain't a complete idiot."

"She let herself get engaged to you, didn't she?"

"Now see here, Breslau!"

"Go to hell," Breslau growled, and pounced two at a time up the stairs of a particularly dilapidated hovel at the corner of Wild Court.

"What would she be doing here?" Nigel demanded, looking with aversion at the dust-grimed hallway. His nostrils pinched at the stench. It smelled for the world like the barn at home when the ewes were in heat.

Breslau didn't bother knocking at Mr. Halton's door. He threw it open, his fingers already curling into fists and his eyes shooting fire. His expression froze when he saw Pamela and Mr. Halton sitting side by side on the sofa with their feet on a table, having a glass of wine and a cheroot, as comfortable as mice in a hole.

"Ah, evening, Breslau, Raleigh," Pamela said, still

using Mr. Ryder's voice. "How the deuce did you find me? Allow me to present Mr. Halton."

"Gentlemen." Mr. Halton smiled, but soon turned a questioning eye on Mr. Ryder. "How *did* they find you, Mr. Ryder?" he asked.

Pamela gave a throaty chuckle. "Breslau's my guardian, you must know. A regular Argus. He has me followed. All right, Breslau, I'm coming. You caught me dead to rights this time. No harm in it after all. Just blowing a cloud and having a few wets with Mr. Halton."

Nigel opened his lips to protest. "Stifle it," Breslau said with a glare that would cut steel. "We must leave now, Mr. Ryder," he said to Pamela.

She removed her feet from the table, set down her cheroot and emptied her wineglass in one gulp. "I suppose we must. Thanks awfully, Halton. I appreciate your hospitality. You must call on me at Breslau House one of these days. I am putting up with my guardian. I look forward to that cock fight."

Breslau directed a daunting look at Mr. Halton. "Mr. Ryder will be returning to the country tomorrow morning. Good night, Mr. Halton."

Civil bows were exchanged, and the company left. Pamela knew instinctively that attack was her best defense. "What wretched timing," she scolded. "I could have got the truth out of him if you hadn't interrupted. A few glasses of wine would have loosened his tongue."

"Just how many glasses did you have?" Nigel demanded.

"One. I dumped the first one behind the sofa when Halton went to get the cheroots. I hadn't

193

time to work the conversation around to Fleur. I had to calm his suspicions when he caught me following him."

"How, pray, did you manage to do that?" Nigel asked.

She hunched her shoulders. "I managed to scrape an acquaintance in front of the theater. I told him I had no friends in town. I had slipped away from my guardian, and followed him in the hope he might accompany me to a tavern. He suggested I go to his place instead."

"And you *went!*" Nigel howled.

As they hurried toward the theater, she became aware that Breslau hadn't said a word since leaving. She had expected a few flesh wounds to show his concern, but all he did was glare. The merciless pace he set left her winded. Were it not for his hand on her elbow, dragging her along, she could not have kept up with him. His lips were set in a grim line, and his jaw was clenched.

"I'll tell you, Pam," Nigel said in a sneering manner, "I'm not at all happy with tonight's work. What would Mama say if she found out what you were up to? Dressing up in my clothes is bad enough. I won't have my fiancée smoking."

A nerve in Breslau's jaw jumped and his hold on her elbow tightened painfully. Pam deemed it a good time to change the subject. "Did anything happen at the theater?" she asked Breslau.

His patience broke just as they turned the corner to Drury Lane. "Never mind trying to divert me. You have behaved outrageously, Miss Comstock, and are very well aware of it. We shall discuss this when we get home."

Nigel chose that inauspicious moment to reassert his claims on Miss Comstock. "Now I think of it, I'm not sure I want Pam staying with you. I'll take you around to Fosters', Pam."

"We can't possibly go to Fosters' at this hour of the night."

"Well, first thing tomorrow morning. If you want to go anywhere, you can call your brother Harley. I shall be busy polishing off the memoirs."

Pam glanced at Breslau. His clenched jaw told her nothing. When they entered the theater, Breslau accompanied them to his box and sat like a statue throughout the remainder of the performance. As the last applause died away, he turned to Pamela.

"I'll call my carriage to take you home," he said in a voice like ice.

"I'm taking Pam to the greenroom," Nigel announced. "Why else do you think she's wearing that monkey suit?"

Pam bit her lip and stared at Breslau. Rather than detract from her appearance, the masculine attire enhanced her femininity. The pale oval of her face was highlighted by the severe hairdo. While she feigned a look of pleading, he knew she would attend the greenroom, with or without his approval. Why should he play the ogre?

His face first thawed, then a soft smile invaded his eyes. In the shadows, he reached for her fingers and squeezed them.

"Very well, but there will be a price to pay," he warned. "And you disobeyed an express order in my note." His eyes slid to Nigel. "You were to divest yourself of a puppy, not acquire yet another."

"Be forewarned, milord. I have a great aversion to following orders. Try a request next time."

"Or perhaps—a proposal?"

In the darkness, his hand moved to grasp her fingers.

Chapter Thirteen

Breslau led the way through the milling throng after the play was finished. Pamela and Nigel followed him along corridors and around corners, down a flight of stairs till they reached the infamous greenroom. At first glance the scene resembled any polite party. The gentlemen were of the first stare, the ladies well-gowned, and the room elegant. The first indication that it was not an ordinary party was the rush of newspapermen who ran to greet Breslau. They each carried a pencil and a notepad, and they flung questions at his head so violently that he automatically fell back.

"Any word on the Flawless Fleur?"

"What is the name of your new production?"

"Is Rose Flanders to play the lead?"

"Is it true Fleur was murdered by French spies?"

Breslau listened politely and smiled. When the reporters fell silent, he said, "No one has offered you a glass of wine, gentlemen. Pray, allow me." He lifted his arm and snapped his fingers. "I shall be making my announcement at midnight."

This only brought forth another volley of questions. "Here is Miss Flanders," Breslau said, and the crowd of black jackets went off in pursuit of Rose.

Pamela pulled at Breslau's elbow and said, "Did you learn anything about Fleur?"

"I know all I have to know about Fleur. It is already eleven-thirty. Just be a little patient, Pamela. And if I may make a suggestion, please lower your voice. It sounds dammed odd to hear a lady's accents issue from a gentleman's mouth."

Nigel scowled. "It sounds worse to hear her do her imitation of her father. Why don't you just sit in a corner and be quiet, Pam? I'll bring you a glass of wine."

Nigel went off for the wine. Breslau lifted a brow and smiled. "For once, I agree with the puppy."

A pretty redheaded ingenue who had been unsuccessfully trying her hand with Breslau for some weeks decided to turn her wiles on the young lad with him, in hopes of access to Breslau. When she came forward and put a possessive hand on Pamela's arm, accompanied by a smile Pamela could only call wanton, Miss Comstock decided a dark corner was the safest place after all. Breslau, his blue eyes dancing, detained the redhead while Pamela made good her escape.

The next half hour was not without interest, even to an observer stuck in the corner with Nigel Raleigh and ordered to be silent. The forward behavior of the actresses and gentlemen who courted them required the vocabulary of a Lady Raleigh to do it justice. Such words as rackety behavior soon escalated to lechery. Rattle turned to rake, actress to light skirt. Pamela watched entranced, looking from time to time to Breslau. The reporters darted from actress to actor, and back to him. She observed that Breslau's main interest centered on the doorway, obviously waiting for some new arrival. Equally obvious, the new arrival was to be Fleur, or someone with news of her.

Pamela didn't have to monitor the door. Nigel did that. If his father suffered a relapse from morality and came to the greenroom, he meant to beat a hasty retreat. When the witching hour arrived, the reporters crowded around Breslau, demanding the promised announcement.

He mounted a chair—perhaps as it was impossible to see the door from the floor—and began a rambling dissertation on the history of Drury Lane. Those who were interested in its history already knew its origins as the Theatre Royale under Thomas Killigrew. When Breslau began telling about Nell Gwyn's debut there, the crowd grew restless.

"He always goes into that spiel when he's stalling for time," Nigel said. "Why don't he announce that I'm dramatizing Fleur's life? That would silence them."

"He called the reporters here," Pam frowned. "He must have something real to tell them."

"My play is real!"

"I'm sure he expected to have news about Fleur by now. That's what they want to know."

"He don't know any more than we do. What we ought to have done is beat the story out of Halton."

Pamela emitted a startled squeal. "Why didn't he? He didn't ask Mr. Halton a *single* question!" While she mused on this, the throng's restlessness took on an angry tinge.

"Fleur! What happened to Fleur?" someone shouted.

That was what they really wanted to hear, but Breslau hoped to forestall chaos by announcing his new play. "Next week we shall begin rehearsing a brilliant new comedy by—"

"Fleur! Fleur! Where is Fleur?"

"The marquise! Flawless Fleur!"

Breslau felt like Daniel in the lion's den, but there was no angel to assist him. Once again he turned a harried gaze toward the door. While he stared, a bizarre apparition entered the doorway and made a melodramatic pause. Trust Fleur. Her timing was exquisite, as usual. Her costume suggested that she had taken considerable pains with this role. What rare and wonderful surprise was hidden beneath her heavy black veil? Why was her left arm in a sling? Why did she look as though she'd been rolling around in a stable? Her tattered outfit of unrelieved black suggested she was playing a widow. But then Fleur always looked well in black. He felt every assurance that she would play her part to the hilt.

"Gentlemen, the Flawless Fleur," Breslau announced with a wave of his arm to the doorway and a bow to his leading lady.

Pamela shrieked every bit as loud as the rest of the audience. "Fleur! She's here, Nigel! Come!"

They both sprang up and ran for a good view. Nigel was lost in the crowd, but Mr. Ryder wiggled her way to the front to hear every word. She watched, mesmerized, while Fleur lifted her elegant white hand and drew aside her veil. Pamela stared for one brief moment at an eye ringed in black. Over the left eye there was a smear of something red that was a fair facsimile of blood. A peek was all anyone had before the veil fell once more over the flawless face.

Pamela expected a clamor of questions, but Fleur had her audience in the palm of her hand. The press scribbled, the caricaturists sketched, and Lord Breslau stood with folded arms, enthralled. In the silence, Pamela examined Fleur's costume. The black gown had a long rent at the left shoulder. A glimpse of white skin peeped enticingly out. The skirt was muddied and ragged around the bottom. What on earth had happened to the marquise? It wasn't the badger sett that had done the damage. That wasn't the gown Fleur wore when she disappeared from Belmont.

At last Fleur opened her mouth and spoke. Her voice was low-pitched, but every syllable was audible in the farthest corner.

"Behold, a miracle. I am Lady Lazarus, risen from the dead. They left me for dead, my body covered with straw in a hay wain carrying me toward Dover."

That, Pamela assumed, accounted for the wisps of straw that still clung to her skirts. She must have glued them. Such were Fleur's dramatic powers that no one enquired who "they" were. To forestall any interruption of her soliloquy, Fleur immediately went on to reveal "them."

"They" were French spies who had broken into her apartment in the country house where she had gone to find a moment's quiet to finish her memoirs. For many years she had been inopportuned by them, but her loyalty was with Britain, where the Prince of Wales himself had thrown his mantle over her when she arrived on Britain's shore, a homeless, derelict noblewoman, cast out of her own country by the rabble.

When she refused to spy for the French, they had determined to drag her to Paris and execute her as a traitor. With God's help and her own bravery, she had recovered sufficiently to escape the hay wain and crawl through mud to the safety of a shepherd's hut, from whence she had made her way back home to Drury Lane.

Breslau clapped louder than the rest. He ably diverted questions that might prove embarrassing by shepherding Fleur out the door and up to his private office to "recover."

"I shall return," Fleur announced from the doorway.

As soon as they were out the door, she clamped a sapient eye on Breslau. Her faltering voice had firmed to ice. "And we shall see who is to be the star of *The Amazing Invalid*, sir. Rose Flanders indeed!"

Pamela squeezed her way to the door and followed. She fully expected to be shut out, but Breslau motioned her to the corner of his office, and Fleur didn't seem to mind having a small addition to her audience. She angrily pulled her left arm from the sling.

"Mees Calmstock! Has he turned you into a player as well?" she asked, staring at the breeches.

"That is another story. We are more interested in hearing yours, Fleur," Breslau said. "The truth, this time, if you please."

Fleur threw back her veil, revealing the black eye and bloodied brow to have been created from makeup. "My story can wait. How dare those scurrilous critics say Rose Flanders can act! She's no actress, and she has played six roles to prove it. Her voice squawks like an unoiled hinge. You called this gathering tonight to announce her in the lead for *The Amazing Invalid*. Don't deny it, monster."

"You know the old saw, Fleur. The show must go on."

"So much for loyalty! Perhaps I should have spied for the French after all. Max, Spiedel—they are all unfaithful." The powerful voice added a vibrato on the last syllables.

Breslau felt an urge to clap. He sat down and folded his arms. As he was attending a performance, it wasn't encumbent on him to remain on his feet. "Where have you been?" he asked.

"What are you paying her? That insipid, simpering—*Anglaise!*"

"No contract has been signed. Come now, you'll have to tell me the truth sooner or later. You tell me where you've been, and I'll tell you whether or not your plan has worked."

"Ass! Of course it hasn't worked. Max running straight to Lady Margaret for comfort. Let him, what do I care? If a mistress-ship is all I'm good for, I could have that from a duke or a prince inside of a week. Let Mr. Spiedel trot the boards of Covent Garden. He'll learn soon enough what a life he's pitched himself into. As to you giving Rose Flanders my role! Ha, she's only a novelty. She won't last a week. You'll come begging to me to save your bacon." A defiant smile parted her lips, and silvery laughter tinkled in a shower around them.

Pamela leaned closer. Fleur disdained to have a seat. She strode back and forth as she spoke, arms waving.

"You want my story? You shall have it. To begin,

I was not quite determined to disappear when I went to Belmont, though I took certain precautions in case it should prove necessary. I left Maria behind, and brought only the necessities with me. It was Max's pusillanimous behavior that decided me. His mother might live for decades. I will not wait on her death to become respectable. The plan was there, in abeyance, *vous comprenez?*"

"*Absolument.*"

"I arranged with a friend, Mr. Halton, to have a carriage waiting in case I required it. He will do anything for money, that one, even make love to Meg Crispin. My butler drove it. Halton was to be in touch with me at the assembly. I told him to bring the carriage around to the side road. He made a scouting expedition a few days earlier, and we chose a spot close to a little spinney."

"We know the place," Breslau nodded. "I rather wondered that you knew Sir Aubrey raised sheep. Halton told you?"

She nodded. "A little slip, that, but no one seemed to notice. I went for a walk before dinner and discovered an old raincoat and galoshes at the rear vestibule. You recall the weather was uncertain. Sable dislikes the wet, and my slippers were nearly new. After the assembly, I left Belmont to meet Mr. Halton, and when I was halfway to the spinney, I remembered I had left something behind."

"Max's glove, or Lady Raleigh's diamond bracelet?"

Fleur gave a squinting look at these interruptions. "The glove. Max left it at my apartment one evening, and I kept it in case I should require an excuse to be in touch with him after one of our squabbles. I brought it with me quite by accident. I thought Lady Raleigh might leap to the conclusion I had been entertaining a gentleman if she saw a man's glove in my room with my lingerie, so I went back for it."

"And the bracelet?"

She gave a Gallic toss of her impertinent shoulders. "A little pourboire. I merely reminded Sir Aubrey of all we had been to each other, and he wanted me to have it for old times' sake. Naturally I didn't leave *that* behind! When I went back for the glove, Nigel came tapping at my door. I didn't want to waste time talking about the memoirs, so I lay down and thought he would think I was asleep. In the confusion, I forgot the bracelet. I heard him gasp—in fact he reached out and touched it. He noticed I was cold from being outdoors. I listened at the door when he left and heard the idiot announce to you that I was dead, if you please." She laughed a mirthless laugh.

"That was when the inspiration struck me! I had planned only to be kidnapped by French spies and turn up after Max and Spiedel had had time to consider how abominably they had treated me. And after the papers had made a great brouhaha about it, of course," she added calmly.

"You will appreciate the value of free publicity, Wes. But then I said, Why not repay Max for his cowardice? Let them think I am dead, and let him have the experience of being under a cloud of suspicion. Let him see how it feels to be despised by society when you are innocent. As I returned to the spinney, I fell into a hole and twisted my ankle. I lay there an age, till finally Halton came and rescued me. 'What is this?' he asked. 'It looks like a bloody grave.' He is a city-bred lad, you know. He thinks milk comes from a jug. And that is when I decided where I should leave Max's glove and my shawl. The shawl, to confirm that both Max and I had been there."

"Very clever. But why did you invent the story about your good-luck shawl in the first place?"

"For effect. I had planned to drop it in the spinney to show where the kidnappers had taken me away. A few clues to keep the newspapermen happy and give the account of my disappearance more length. I tossed a handkerchief into the bushes as well."

"The badger sett had the corners squared. When did you do that?"

"Another inspiration. Someone had been digging there before. Sealing up the hole, I think. I was afraid the wretched little beasts would crawl out and bite me, but I noticed the entrance had been filled in with earth."

"Nigel said something about his mother having the holes filled up. The badgers were after her honey," Pamela said from the corner. "But there was fresh digging, and a shovel there."

"I had seen the shovel when I was looking for a raincoat and galoshes for my flight," Fleur explained. "My gown was destroyed when I fell in the hole, and after I was in the carriage, I had to send Halton back for my things. Rather than decide what I needed, I told him to pick up the lot. He brought the shovel back to the badger sett as well and enlarged the hole. He was supposed to return the shovel to Belmont when he took back the raincoat and galoshes, but I assume he forgot it. I trust he hid the coat and galoshes. I didn't want Sir Aubrey involved."

"They came to light, but it's no matter," Breslau said.

Pamela risked another question. "Where did you have Mr. Halton take you when you left? We've looked at your apartment, and Mr. Spiedel's, and Mr. Halton's."

"I was with friends," she said vaguely.

"In Kent, actually," Breslau added with an arch smile at the marquise.

"Well, there is no necessity to hide it from you, Wes. I joined the Coventry players at Chatham. But how did you know? We took the most impossible route from Belmont, over mere cattle trails, so no one would see us."

"When you weren't in London, I scanned the itinerary of the traveling players. People usually go home during times of crisis. You have told me more than once that other actors are your real family. Those at Chatham were the closest. Naturally you would want to be near enough that you could read of your disappearance in the newspapers the day they were printed."

"I even knew Tuck's players were there!" Pamela exclaimed. "I saw them perform *The Beggar's Opera.*"

"And survived? I compliment you, Mees Calmstock. So you weren't fooled by my little trick?" the marquise asked, turning to Breslau.

"I own I was confused—for a while. How long did you plan to remain away?"

"Not past Saturday. You didn't think I'd let Rose have the busiest night of the week! Her sudden rise to eminence hastened my return," she added with an astringent look. "Did you plan to announce her as your leading lady tonight?"

"Only if you failed my summons, Fleur. I thought those announcements might bring you back."

Her fine eyes flashed with fire. "It was all a trick? You haven't offered Rose the part?"

"Not yet."

"And the other announcement—Max?" she asked hopefully.

"Lady Margaret is visiting friends in Surrey. Max is desolate at his own laggardly behavior. You might get a proper offer, if you play your hand carefully."

"I hardly dare to ask ... John—Mr. Spiedel?" Fleur's theatrical manner deserted her. It was genuine concern that glowed in her eyes now. "Is it true he's going to Covent Garden?"

"Your son has various avenues suddenly open to him."

"Ah, you figured out he is my son. You are too clever for me, Wes. What an abominable husband he will make you, Mees Calmstock. You should do as I planned to do, and marry a foolish man. So much more comfortable. Well, it is only fair Spiedel's father do something for him. I admit I have been active on his behalf. Which one—"

"Three, to date. He tells me Sir Aubrey has offered him cash, Lord Alban a position."

"A position? He usually gives cash."

"Yes, a fair bit of it over the past six months. Mr. Spiedel hasn't seen much of it, has he?" Breslau asked. "A Mr. Webb is also eager to do something for the lad. What have you against his going into the theater, Fleur? It's done pretty well by you."

"You call this well?" she asked with a haughty stare. "Having to trick a man like Maxwell to marry me? I, a marquise? In England, the stage is not respectable. It is otherwise in France, where people have a proper understanding of the theater. But then the stage there is enobled by such geniuses as Racine and Corneille."

"You omit the great comic writer, Molière," Breslau added with a laughing eye.

"Back to your old hobbyhorse. I will not be limited to comic roles, Breslau. Did tonight's performance not show you I am capable of greater things?"

"You have an undeniable talent for melodrama."

"For tragedy! Which is not to say I couldn't be persuaded to do *The Amazing Invalid*, if the price is right . . ." She looked a question at him.

"I might convince the directors to go as high as thirty-five."

"Siddons got fifty. I couldn't accept less than forty-five."

"Forty it is," he agreed, with a good understanding of Fleur's strategy.

"And a promise of a tragedy for my next role."

"Your next role will be Lady Chamaude. Nigel is hot at the task. It is for you to decide whether that is tragedy or farce."

"My life? He stole that from my memoirs! He won't get away with it."

"Royalties to be hammered out before production."

The marquise wore a pensive look. "My life should be dramatized. It is true I've had a very—dramatic existence. As to tragedy or farce—it is reality, Wes. We shall advertise it as theatrical realism. By the by, I shan't take a sou less than fifty percent of the royalties. Raleigh will rifle my book for his dialogue. I have a great deal of unforgettable dialogue in the memoirs. What lines I wrote for the Prince Regent!"

"That will be for you and Raleigh to decide with the publisher. I have only one other stipulation. No more blackmail, Fleur."

"Blackmail? You mistake the matter. Each of my gentlemen friends was in alt to hear he had fathered a son. Men are such egotists. I demanded nothing. I merely went and gave a performance that showed how much I had done for our son, and how little the father. All my friends were gentlemen, sir. No blackmail was necessary."

"Sir Aubrey appeared less than happy."

"No, only less than wealthy. I could have made something of the man, had I met him before he was married to his Methodist. It is fitting that John have a chance in life."

"Perhaps you're right, but he has his chance now. No more blackmail. And now it is time to rejoin the gentlemen from the press. Better put on your veil. The kohl on your eyes is running."

Fleur drew out a handkerchief and mirror and attended to this detail. "Did my disappearance cause much disturbance at Belmont?"

"Not as much as the disappearance of Lady Raleigh's bracelet. Sir Aubrey will want to buy it back, I fancy. He's at the Reddleston Hotel now."

"What is he doing here?"

"He came to see Mr. Spiedel. Who is Spiedel's father, Fleur? Do you know?"

Fleur gave a Gallic shrug. "It's difficult to say. But

210

I know who his mother is. He'll not want while I am alive."

"He doesn't know he's your son?"

"I was afraid he'd want to follow my footsteps into the theater if I told him. I had him adopted by friends, the Spiedels, to hide his illegitimacy, but I have always kept close to him. Since his coming to London, we have grown closer. He thinks I am a friend of his mama's."

She stopped at the doorway. The aura of the actress fell away again, and she looked like a worried, lonesome woman. "Do you think I should let him join the theater? He has great talent, you know. The theater hasn't done so badly by me."

"Would you really want to be in any other line of work?"

She shook her head. "No, with all its ups and downs, there is no life like it," she said musingly. "There is a part in *The Amazing Invalid*—the heroine's younger brother . . . It might make a suitable debut for John. The role would have to be padded. He only gets a dozen lines."

"That's not impossible."

"I wouldn't want him to go to the Garden. We would end up rivals. It would be such a pleasure to work with him, to teach him the subtle nuances—he tends to rant when the lines require no more than a whisper. An amateur's failing—you know what I mean. It is the way Rose Flanders played Emily tonight. It would be such a consolation to me to have him near. Yes, I'll do it," she decided.

Her harried air fell away, and a smile of relief seized her mobile countenance. "He'll be another Garrick! A Kean! Kemble is nothing to him. Let me

211

tell him, Wes." An expression of noble grief replaced the smile. She was back in her role of the Flawless Fleur. "If I can't tell him I'm his mother, let me play Lady Bountiful at least."

On this sad speech, she turned toward the door.

"You forgot your sling!" Pamela called.

"You *ruined* my exit!"

After the door had slammed, Pamela sighed. "Isn't she wonderful?"

"Flawless."

"She would be wasting her time to marry Maxwell."

"She won't marry him. She may accept an engagement to lend her respectability, and to have the pleasure of jilting him. Since she's going to let Spiedel go on the stage, I believe this lust for respectability will fade. It was for him she wanted it really."

"I can't imagine why anyone would want to be respectable when she could be an actress instead. How did you figure out that Fleur was just playing off a stunt?"

"The escapade smelled suspicious from the start. There was no evidence of violence in her departure. No body in the grave, yet no one seemed to have come along to prevent burial. The Maxwells saw the carriage but didn't go into the spinny. Why not use the grave then, since it was dug? The grave began to look like a stage prop, no more."

"And that called to mind Fleur."

"After a process of elimination, it began to look that way. Maxwell obviously knew nothing, Sir Aubrey appeared innocent—of murder, I mean," he added with a laughing eye. "Halton, who spirited her away, was a friend, with no reason to kidnap or

murder her. There was no demand for ransom—
fancy Fleur forgetting that! But then the Frenchies
weren't after money, only Fleur to carry home for a
trophy."

"She has a wonderful bent for fiction."

"It comes from practice. Her whole life since leaving France is laced with fiction. Anyway, it began to
look like a voluntary disappearance. Her maid was
too ill to accompany her to Belmont, but had recovered amazingly the next day. Her butler was missing. When I had a description from Newman's two
hours ago of the man driving the rig, I felt confident
I was on the right track. And she was furious with
Max at the assembly. I knew she'd wreak some re-
venge on him. When I realized she wanted to pressure certain parties to do certain things . . ."

"Spiedel not to go on the stage, and Maxwell to
marry her . . ."

"Also the alleged fathers to feel remorse for having neglected their son. She didn't mention that, but
it was bound to tweak their consciences when they
read of her disappearance. And let us not forget
Breslau. She wanted me to give her a raise, and a
crack at tragedy."

"The funny thing is, her plan worked, but—I mean
she's going to let Spiedel go on the stage after all.
And you don't think she'll marry Maxwell. All she
really got is ten guineas more for a performance.
Speidel's the one who profited more."

Breslau reached down and lifted a piece of straw
that had attached to his jacket. "Ten guineas per
performance ain't hay. It adds up. I hope the publicity draws enough people to cover the extra expense.
Helping Speidel wouldn't weigh lightly with Fleur.

He is the one person outside of herself she truly cares for. But the stunt did more good than that. It has made Fleur take a good hard look at her life, and decide what role she really wants to play."

"The one I feel sorry for is Rose Flanders. She thinks she's going to have the lead in *The Amazing Invalid*."

"Cut to the quick that you could think so badly of me, Pamela. Rose is to have the lead in a light farce we're working on. Settling that was one of my errands this morning when I left you at home to read the newspaper. Rose confirmed that Fleur has friends in Tuck's players. Halton's mentioning Kent to Meg Crispin made me look in that direction. Rose's new role is to be announced tonight as well."

"Surely that didn't take all day. What were you and Maxwell doing the rest of the time?"

"Max mentioned writing to his mama about marrying Fleur. Such a composition will take him an age. I made a quick dart to Chatham."

"To confirm that Fleur was with Tuck's players?"

Breslau gave her a surprised look. "That, too. It's been a busy day."

"It's not quite over yet."

"I am aware of that." A glow entered his eyes. "The best is yet to come."

Pamela felt the warmth of his glow and said in confusion, "Should we not go back to the greenroom?"

"Let us give Fleur her solo moment of glory. We don't want an audience for what we have to discuss, Pamela." He sat beside her, frowning at her masculine getup.

"The excitement is all over then," she said sadly,

peering hopefully from the corner of her eyes. "Tomorrow I shall go to Fosters'."

"It tugs at the heartstrings to see you relegated to such respectability."

"You don't have a heart!"

"I do, but there are strings attached." He drew the tie from her hair and flung it aside. "It's hard enough trying to propose to a lady wearing breeches. At least let us see your hair."

"*Propose*? Breslau!"

"I am not so lacking in propriety as you imagine. I mentioned going to Chatham ... Your papa was uncommonly relieved to receive a firm offer for you. Oh, and your mama sent along the rose gown. I see *that* cheers you up."

He looked hopefully to hear her proclaim the true cause of that bewitching smile that possessed her. "Papa cannot know you are involved in the theater if he gave his permission."

"I wore the face reserved for relatives. Actually he has no idea *you* harbor a thespian streak, either. I know you would prefer being an actress to dull respectability, but I assure you it is not dull respectability I am offering." His fingers rested on the warm nape of her neck, and began massaging it with suspicious expertise. When the tension left her neck, his fingers moved to her hair, stroking, curling it round his fingers. While his hands performed these intimate familiarities, his voice cajoled her. "The theater is part of my life. It will be part of yours as well, if you'll have me."

She swallowed convulsively. Her eyes blinked in belated astonishment. "I never gave a minute's thought to marrying you. How could I possibly?" Her voice was breathless and uncertain.

His head inclined toward hers, and his voice lowered to a whisper. "If it is your indeterminate sort of half engagement to Nigel . . ."

"I wouldn't let that stop me!"

"Nor I." His lips hovered above hers, just brushing them. "He mentioned you have chosen the church."

"Ye—" He silenced her with a kiss that began as a tentative touch and increased to passion as his arms crushed her to him.

His assault stirred visions of a delightfully disreputable future. It was obvious a man who kissed like Lord Breslau had no notion of respectability. Pamela forgot all her mother's injunctions of the proper behavior of a young lady as she returned every scandalous embrace.

It was several moments later that Pamela sat with her head resting on Breslau's shoulder. "Someone will have to tell Nigel," she murmured.

"I've already told him."

She smiled softly. "What did he say?"

"Kiss me."

"An odd thing to say to *you*! He never said it to *me*!"

"Now!"

"Never once, now that I consider it."

"Pamela!"

"Don't be such a gudgeon, Wes. This is no time for lovemaking. Let us go to the greenroom."